the PHANTOM ROAN

by STEPHEN HOLT

**SBS** **SCHOLASTIC BOOK SERVICES**
New York Toronto London Auckland Sydney

To the Memory of My Beloved
MOTHER

*   *   *

Copyright 1949 by Stephen Holt. This edition is published by Scholastic Book Services, a division of Scholastic Magazines, Inc., by arrangement with Longman's Green and Co., Inc.

7th printing . . . . December 1968
Printed in the U.S.A.

CONTENTS

• Born in western Kansas, Stephen Holt moved with his family at an early age to Nebraska. When he was eight the family moved again to the T.X. ranch at Spring Coulee, in Alberta, Canada, near the Blood Indian Reservation. His high school years were spent at Calgary Collegiate Institute and in South Pasadena, California. After graduation he enrolled in the University of Southern California at Los Angeles.

Stephen Holt learned to ride when he was three, and at six was riding the lead horse for the reapers during the harvest. After college, he went into advertising. He lives in San Marino, California, is married, and has a son and two daughters.

1. Trouble

GLENN BARNES moved to the log-barn door, averting his eyes from Roy H's empty stall. To hide the hurt within him, he took hold of the broken hasp on the door, rattling it a time or two.

"Shucks," he managed to whisper, "some horses have to die of colic. Harmon of the *Double Anchor* says so." Moving easily, he walked to a little niche beside the feed box and, getting a hammer, started to nail the hasp back on. Working, he kept his eyes from roving out to the rolling Alberta hills that would remind him of the sleek bay horse. The hills over which he and Roy H had raced, but would never race again. For Roy H was gone.

Old Lucifer Barnes, his foster father, big, and with a soft voice constant as the west wind blowing down from the Rockies off to the southwest, came from the dark interior of the barn.

"You must be feeling this something fierce, Glenn," he said, throwing a heavy arm around the boy's shoulders.

Glenn drew a nail from the hasp and, straightening it with two blows of his hammer, drove it back into its place.

He swung around then, touching Luce's arm. Luce,

1

he thought, must be feeling the loss of Roy H as much as he. "It's just as tough for you," he said gently.

Walter Swanson, Glenn's foster uncle, who was small and fair with shrewd blue eyes, came up to join them. He was manager of a bank in Lethbridge and was used to handling situations. His manner said that he could handle this one, too.

"You go on up to the house, Glenn," he said, firmly grasping his arm. "Luce and I'll take over here."

Glenn paused. How easy it would be to let Uncle Walter and Luce take over. But suddenly he squared his shoulders and shook his head. No, sir, he wasn't dodging anything. Besides, he wanted to pick the spot where Roy H would lie out under the cotton-wood tree beside the path leading to the river, close to its murmur and the wind in the willows along its banks.

"I'm all right," he said, and turned to go with Luce and Uncle Walter. They went toward the back of the barn and on to the lot.

As he walked, Glenn found Uncle Walter beside him. "You know, Glenn," he said crisply, "you'd better pull out of here."

Glenn did not slacken his pace. To leave all this, the little ranch house on the edge of the Old Man River, and the ranch itself with its ten square miles of the best grazing land in Alberta!

"I'll think it over," he promised and walked on.

They reached the pasture lot and Glenn peeled off his windbreaker and shirt, then picked up a shovel.

It wasn't until the June sun stood directly over-head that Glenn, resisting an impulse to turn for a last look, walked back to the barn. Uncle Walter was beside him.

Glenn kept silent, hiding the ache, for now that he might have to leave, the ranch had become very precious indeed.

Glenn knew that he musn't indulge himself. He'd have to have "sand," the same stuff that Roy H had always had—that had carried him through any emergency with something to spare at the end of a long day's ride.

He wasn't a boy any longer.

They reached the barn and Uncle Walter's sharp appraising eyes took in the eight drying cowhides folded across the top pole of the corral.

"Well, Glenn," he said, "I guess you're pretty well washed up here on the *Shoestring* ranch."

Glenn stared at the hides too. These represented the end of the *Shoestring* herd. There was nothing left to bring in money.

He nodded. "Yes, guess so."

Uncle Walt moved closer, his eyes brightening with a persuasive gleam.

"I can give you a job as teller," he said. "You'll be somebody." His eyes fell appraisingly on Luce's shambling form going into the barn.

Glenn paused to scan Uncle Walt's sharp canny face, so different from the kindly impractical one of Luce. He didn't want to take the job, but it offered a way out. It would force him to leave the ranch but it would give him a chance to send money back to Luce.

Sure, Luce would miss him and Aunt Abbie too. And he would miss them, and the story which he never tired hearing them tell. How one morning, eighteen years before, or a little less, Luce had heard a car stop at daylight, followed by a knock on the door, then a car driving away.

"Presently, we heard a baby cry," Luce said. "And Abbie says, 'You better go see, Luce.' I went to the front door and opened it and there you were in a little basket, red-faced and bawling and fighting that pink blanket with a pair of husky fists."

Glenn came back to Uncle Walt. No use trying to make him see how he felt about leaving this ranch and Luce and Abbie.

"It would give me ready money," he agreed.

"Sure thing. Now you're being practical and smart."

Glenn knew that he would have to send the money to Luce. If he sent it to Aunt Abbie she would just turn it over to Luce, anyway.

"Luce handles the money," she always declared. "What happens outside is his business. My work is in this house."

She had always been that way, steadfast and strong, making the best baking-powder biscuits this side of Calgary, refusing to interfere as Lucifer brought the once prosperous *Shoestring* down, and down still further with his kind-hearted but foolish spending, scorning to feel sorry for herself.

The bookcases were lined with sets of encyclopedias from young salesmen working their way through college. And there was that sea-water contraption in the woodshed that Luce was waiting to take to Vancouver, "to turn ocean water sweet and make a fortune."

Glenn stirred, feeling his uncle's presence, the brisk, crisp way he just stood there, waiting. Again came that sudden hollowness within Glenn at the thought of leaving the *Shoestring*.

He took hold of the barn door, and the hills around him seemed to roll with him.

"Come on," he told himself. "Let's cut out the sob stuff." Thrusting out his chin and squaring his broad shoulders, he followed Uncle Walt toward the little unpainted house east of the barn.

Abigail did not look up as Glenn and Uncle Walter came in. It was so like her to let him take the lead.

Straight as a pine, she stood before the kitchen table, sleeves rolled up, hands and arms firm and hard at sixty, moving rhythmically back and forth rolling out biscuits.

"Dinner will be ready in a few minutes, men," she said.

Glenn did not miss the way she said, "men." It was Abbie's quiet way of telling him that what he did was strictly up to him; that he was free to make his own decisions.

He moved to get a drink of water from the pail by the kitchen window, waiting for what he knew was coming from Uncle Walter. He would give Uncle Walter every chance, and not dodge the issue of whether he should go to Lethbridge and work in Uncle Walter's bank.

Uncle Walter sat down in a straight pine chair and, leaning back against the wall, said, "I've been telling Glenn that he ought to pull out."

Glenn watched Abbie's strong spare face, remembering how she'd helped him through school, kept his clothes clean, watching over him yet never saying "you do this, for I think it best."

Could it be, Glenn wondered, standing there in the kitchen, that but five weeks ago he had sat with the class at Macleod High School? That he had risen as valedictorian of his class and said to the townspeople, "The best life is the life of healing."

He remembered Abbie's face, there in the fifth row, impassive, but plainly showing her rapt attention and agreement. For Abbie wanted him to be a veterinarian, as much as he wanted to be one. It was a secret dream shared between them. Yes, now but a dream, for there were no cows on the *Shoestring*, and he had to come down to earth and get a job.

"Yes." Glenn nodded. "Uncle Walter's offered me a job in his bank."

In the silence that followed, Glenn didn't expect Abbie to speak. She would feel as he did.

Uncle Walter's voice was saying, "It's a white-collar job, Abbie. It will teach Glenn how to handle money. It will make him somebody in the world." To the sound of Uncle Walter's words and to the gentle movement of Abbie's hands in the biscuit dough, Glenn made his own choice.

He walked into his bedroom and began packing, forcing himself not to glance out to the hills, the river, and all the things he had learned to love and would now have to leave.

He pulled down a battered yellow suitcase and stuffed into it two blue shirts, half a dozen pairs of socks that Abbie had knitted for him, his good blue suit, and a pair of brown shoes. With a lump in his throat, he reached for the blue and red tie Abbie had given him for graduation and the tooled-leather belt from Luce.

His eyes fell on the bookshelf and his textbook on physiology, but he jerked them away. That belonged to the past and had no part in the life of a bank teller.

Closing the lid of the suitcase and straightening his back, smoothing out his frown and mustering a smile, he went empty handed back to the kitchen. This must be harder on Abbie than himself, and it would be time enough after dinner to tell her.

They sat down at the pine table, eating in silence except for the ceaseless hum of Luce's voice, which to them all was silence.

Glenn was thankful for the voice. It left him silent and able to get through the meal of crisp ham, boiled potatoes, and white fluffy sweet-to-the-mouth turnips made so by Abbie's secret of slicing a bit of raw potato in them as they cooked.

He drank the river water, for there was no milk. Their milk cow was one of those whose hides stretched on the corral fence. Well, he'd send money for another cow from his bank wages. Suddenly he rose from the table; there was no use beating about the bush.

"You'll want to take a day or so off," Luce's sighing voice came softly, "before you decide what to do about getting more cows for the *Shoestring*."

Glenn was conscious of Abbie's hands, barely moving yet tightening as they lay in her lap. He shook his head.

"I guess not," he said. "I'm going to work in Uncle Walter's bank."

Glenn saw Luce's head rise slowly, and his eyes meet Abbie's, with a dazed stricken look.

His words, "But, how about being a vet?" were

smothered in the sharp crisp ones of Uncle Walter's, "That's the boy, Glenn. Now you're talking sense. You'll wear a white shirt and handle money. In ten years you'll be a cashier; in twenty, well"—his harsh laugh sounded—"I'm not going to live forever, and the bank will need a new manager."

Glenn went into the bedroom and brought out the suitcase, forcing himself to move briskly.

"I'm not going for a week or so," Walter said.

"I'll catch a ride to Cardston," Glenn said. "Get the Lethbridge bus from there, after I sell my saddle."

"Sell your saddle?" Luce's voice rose then in a stricken whisper.

"Sure," he said. "Pete Offendorfer down by the Cardston bridge said if I ever wanted to let it go he'd give me a hundred dollars for it."

"A hundred dollars is a hundred dollars," Walter Swanson said.

Abbie and Luce did not move. They sat stunned.

In the silence that followed, Glenn went out the door and down to the barn to sack up his saddle, with the steer tooled into the cantle; his lariat, strapped to its bulging tree; and his old worn Navajo blanket. The saddle skirt, ripped by that bronc at Calgary last year when he'd taken second in the saddle-bucking contest, caught on the edge of the burlap bag. Resisting an impulse to stuff it madly in, Glenn gently lifted the saddle, tried again and fitted it into the bag. Then he shouldered it and walked back to the house.

Abbie was by the window that looked out on the jigsaw pattern of the Rockies off to the south and west. The dishes, whisked from the table, lay in a pan of soapy water from which her arms came up to stiff shoulders.

Walter hadn't moved. There was something triumphant in the way he sat in his chair.

Glenn moved across the pine floor to Abbie and gave her a swift peck on the firm hard cheek, then went out to the porch. If he had waited he would never have made it.

Abbie, drying her hands on a towel, followed.

"A little later you could catch the bus," Luce pleaded.

Glenn shook his head. He wanted to go, and fast.

"I'll catch a ride," he said. "Hitchhike with someone coming along the Calgary road." With a swift movement he tossed his saddle across his broad back, then picked up his suitcase.

Uncle Walter said, "I'll telephone Jim West, my cashier, that you're coming."

Glenn nodded. Taking a deep breath, he jumped off the porch and walked toward the highway a half mile to the east.

Luce came with him to where the end of the *Shoestring* corner met the highway. "If I could only do something," he said as they walked along. "Buy some invention that would go like wildfire."

They reached the fence corner. Beyond lay the smooth black-top macadam highway leading to Cardston through Standoff, thence to the Cardston bridge.

"No, Luce," Glenn cautioned, "keep away from inventions and wait for money from me. You can buy a cow and maybe a few calves later on."

Shifting the saddle to an easier thrust on his shoulder, he walked on down the trail to the highway. There he turned and, putting his saddle on the ground beside his yellow suitcase, glanced up the road for a car.

One whizzed past, a California car with a dark-haired girl and a boy laughing as they rode, but they were headed for Calgary.

A second car, coming his way, passed him up, then a third.

At length a Ford light-delivery truck stopped. A farmer with a long smooth face and solemn mouth leaned to open the door, and said, "Hop in, cowboy."

Glenn, after a final look back at Luce standing lonely and immovable beside the fence corner, flung his stuff into the back and climbed in.

Carefully controlling his voice, he said, "Thanks a lot, sir."

"Leavin' home?" the man said, starting the car.

Glenn waited till he could speak naturally. "Yes," he said. The crisp voice of his Uncle Walt came to him. "I'm getting out of here. I'm going to amount to something."

The car started and there was no sound but the whine of the tires on the macadam pulling him along toward Cardston and the bus that would take him to Lethbridge and his new job.

2. The Outlaw

GLENN sat bolt upright in the car, trying not to look at the country, trying to concentrate on the hum of the tires on the pavement and the drone of the man's voice beside him. But every rise in the road brought some memory to stab him. That knoll off to the left had been his place for sitting Roy H, to sweep with his eyes the sealike plain of grass to the west at sunset. An eagle, its huge wings motionless, coasted on the early afternoon breeze high above them. He, too, had been there before.

Glenn stirred in his seat.

"This is no way for a guy to act," he fiercely told himself. "Especially a guy who's going to sell his saddle and wash up on all this for good. A guy who's going to be somebody in a bank."

"You're Luce Barnes' adopted son, ain't you?" the farmer queried, with a sidewise glance.

Glenn knew the custom of the country. The man was just being friendly. He nodded. Luce had stood by him, now Glenn had to make some money fast, to help.

The car moved on and presently the hills around them sharpened, and the road led down into the Belly River coulee. In the distance, at a spot where years be-

fore some white men had withstood a band of attacking Blood Indians, lay the sprawling town of Standoff.

Glenn closed his eyes to shut out the rolling hills
sweeping from the river and the smooth clear water
itself.

Here, right under this bridge across which the car
thundered, he and Roy H had once gone swimming.

Glenn caught his breath with the memory of the
sleek bay horse diving into the deep pool, snorting
and blowing water over him as they swam; the wonder of climbing out from the pool to saddle up and
race off into the twilight for home and the *Shoestring*.
He passed a hand across his eyes, then glanced sideways to see if the driver had noticed.

"Luce bought any inventions lately?" The man's
amused voice came to Glenn. "He'd sure go for something new on perpetual motion."

Glenn couldn't smile with the man, nor blame him.
He was only saying what everybody knew about
Luce, the length of Alberta.

"No," he murmured, wishing the car would step
along. "Guess he hasn't bought anything new."

The Ford chugged up from the river coulee to the
flat land, then headed west toward Cardston. Glenn
tried not to see white-faced cattle as they passed.
They reminded him of the eight hides on the *Shoestring's* corral fence.

A coyote, dun-colored against the hills, slunk from
a draw to howl plaintively on a knoll.

Glenn's midriff tightened. He was going to miss all
this in Lethbridge.

The car moved on, with the man at the wheel trying to get to Glenn. "So, you're going to the city?" he asked, shaking his head sadly.

Glenn stared straight ahead. "Yes," he said. "Going to be a bank teller."

The man nodded.

Silence settled over the moving car.

"Funny." The man shook his head again. "I'd pick you for a country man instead of a city guy. Something to do with animals."

In Glenn's silence, the man turned back to his wheel but he went on talking.

"Now, if you wanted it, I'm pretty sure I could get you a job helping Doc Crane, the Cardston veterinary. There's a job with lots of excitement: helping around the hospital, inspecting dipping vats, maybe tangling with Peters of the *Rolling R* over whether he's going to dip his cattle for mange or not. Peters is not used to being told what to do—says this dipping is all a waste of time—but maybe you can handle him."

Glenn wished he'd skipped this car back there on the Macleod road. He'd be glad when the farmer left him at the bridge—glad when he'd sold his saddle and was in his bus headed for town.

Carefully keeping his voice down, and his eyes straight ahead, Glenn said, "That's good of you, but I'm headed for Lethbridge."

"Okay, okay, it was just an idea."

Silence settled again over the moving car.

The sun, a red ball of fire, dipped behind the blue mountains. An evening breeze blew cool.

The car covered another twenty miles, then turned to swing down along the St. Mary's River that ran cool and like a silver thread between cut-banks lined with cottonwoods and willows. Little islands, cut off by the fury of the stream in spring floods, dotted the stream bed that wound across the prairie.

Here and there stray bands of Indian ponies grazed among the trees or stopped to slake their thirst at the clear stream.

In ten minutes the car approached the St. Mary's bridge. Cardston, a small prairie town, lay two miles to the southwest. Pete Offendorfer's ranch was just beyond the bridge. Glenn had told Uncle Walt, when he'd offered Glenn the bank job, that he would stay there.

Glenn stirred in his seat and, pulling off his Stetson, wiped his damp forehead. He took a deep breath and, still careful to keep his voice level, said, "I'll get off here." Then he added softly, "Thanks for the lift."

The man at the wheel drove the car to the bridge, then pulled it to a halt. Over the side of the car, as Glenn fished for his suitcase and saddle, the man's troubled gray eyes were fixed on him. Something was wrong, that was sure, but he didn't know what.

"Sure you don't want that job with Crane?"

Glenn was dead sure. He didn't want any part of being a veterinarian, or anything that had to do with horses after Roy H.

"Yes, I'm sure," he said, mustering a smile. "And thanks again."

"I'd take you on into town, but my wife's expecting me and I have chores to do."

"Skip it," Glenn protested. "I'll get another ride in."

Glenn stood by the car which did not move, his saddle across his shoulders and his suitcase in his right hand. He guessed he'd better go on to Pete Offendorfer's.

But he heard the low gurgle of the river running under the bridge. A black despair settled down upon him. He knew that he could not go to Pete's right now, nor even on into Cardston to catch the bus for Lethbridge.

In a sort of panic, he straightened under the load of his forty-pound saddle and moved to go down the bank to the river.

"If you're aimin' to foot it along the river bottom," the man said from the car, "watch it. There's a roan outlaw loose hereabouts. A rodeo castoff that hates all men."

Glenn paused. At any other time the idea of fearing a horse would have struck him as very funny—he who had spent his life with horses and ridden in Stampedes from Calgary to Madison Square Garden in New York City!

Now, he just wanted to get away from this wellmeaning farmer and go down by the river. He'd build a fire and stretch out by its warmth. He'd unsack his saddle and, using it for a pillow and his Navajo blanket for a cover, spend one more night free, listening to the river and the sigh of the wind in the trees.

Glenn swung to face the farmer.

"Okay, I'll watch it," he said. "And thanks again."

"Not at all, I just thought I'd warn you. He's an outlaw, shoved off somebody's string to die out there along the river. He's got cropped ears from frostbite. He's branded with a sprawling C on his right thigh, though nobody seems to know the brand."

Glenn thanked the farmer again, watching him

reluctantly start his car and thunder off across the bridge heading east.

"Now," Glenn whispered, "now to make camp. A last camp."

Diving down the bank, he walked along the river to a clump of cottonwoods. He scooped out a place and built a fire of dead cottonwood sticks, then unsacked his saddle and his Navajo blanket.

He tried to eat one of Abbie's sandwiches. It had no taste when he thought of leaving all this for his job at the bank. He fed the remainder of the sandwich to a garrulous crow cawing from a branch just above his head, then lying back with the saddle seat for a pillow, he pulled a mouth organ from his windbreaker pocket. It was an old Hohner harmonica, battered and worn, but Abbie had given it to him.

Lying there, his eyes searching the now darkening sky filled with blinking stars, he began to play a tune that he loved and had learned a note at a time: the *Blue Danube Waltz*. For half an hour he played it, switching to *Home on the Range, The Cowboy's Lament*, but always coming back to *The Blue Danube*.

At length, he stowed the mouth organ away, yawned and closed his eyes.

How long he slept Glenn did not know. When a noise wakened him, there remained only the dull glow of the coals of his wood fire. The moon, high in the sky above him, shone clear and bright. He turned to the sound that had roused him, staring questioningly off into the thicket of willows to his right, then rubbed his eyes and stared again.

A horse stared back at him. In the bright moonlight

he seemed ghostly, unreal, almost a phantom horse. Partly hidden by the trees, he stood silent, specterlike.

"The outlaw!" Glenn breathed, his eyes racing to follow the sprawling *C*, the cropped ears of the horse before him. Glenn gathered himself to spring from a charge, for the horse hated him. He could tell.

The roan stood, head up, nostrils quivering, eyes red in the moonlight.

But suddenly Glenn caught his breath with pity.

The outlaw made a move to charge him, then, because one leg did not touch the ground, swung his muzzle down to it. He made a second dive for Glenn, making a feeble effort to strike. But the agony in his foot stopped him cold.

Glenn moved instinctively to help the horse, but checked himself. He was going to Lethbridge.

"After all, he's not mine," he said, turning back to his saddle.

But the roan waving his foot back and forth in ceaseless pain was something he could not ignore. The wind, low and soft, came whispering along the ground, bringing the roan's nicker of anguish to Glenn.

It broke something down within him.

"Oh, well," he said, and swinging around, moved cautiously toward the outlaw.

The horse, with the memory of a thousand enemy riders searing his mind, laid back his cropped ears and bared his teeth. But a deep instinct suddenly checked his third charge for Glenn. Something within him seemed to prompt, "Here is help!"

Some of the defiance went out of the roan and he waited.

Glenn moved close to lift the injured foot. For a second the odor of the wound rocked him. Then he looked more closely, put the foot down, and moved to build up the fire.

"Now," he said, leading the roan by his mane close to the fire and once more lifting the foot. "I thought so," he muttered at length, gingerly pushing at the frog now swollen almost beyond recognition. "It's a rock in the frog."

He pulled a pocketknife from his Levi's and, opening the largest blade, held it deep in the fire coals to sterilize it. Letting it cool, he steadied the roan's foot.

"Now," he said. "Let's see, boy."

He worked swiftly. Sweat stood out on his forehead. He gagged from the odor. But he worked steadily, forgetting something of his anguish over Roy H and the hateful prospect of his bank job in his absorption. Talking soothingly all the time and working swiftly, he probed for the rock and after a struggle pried it from its pocket imbedded in the roan's foot.

It came free, a three-cornered jagged piece of granite, picked up along the river bed.

"There," Glenn said in triumph, then caught himself. "It was just a rock, just a rock that any kid could have dug out with his pocketknife."

He took his hat and moved down to the river to scoop water into its wide brim to flush out the wound.

"That will clean it out, and now beat it," he said, slapping the roan's flank.

After washing his hands at the river, he came back to his saddle and lay down once more.

But the roan did not move away. He stood there and the pain seemed to die out of his eyes. The fury of hatred was less too.

Glenn turned away from the roan, trying to forget his exhilaration in helping an animal in pain.

"Skip it, Glenn," he said to himself, and closed his eyes tight.

But the roan's presence haunted him, and again came that old dream of his and Abbie's, that he become a veterinarian. And he sat up, recalling that he'd forgotten about Roy H in his concern for the outlaw's foot.

For a long time he sat there, running his hand through his mop of dull-red hair and staring fixedly into the firelight.

Suddenly the roan hobbled to his side.

Glenn, his heart thudding, pulled the feverish head to him. It was a beautiful head, he knew then, small and broad. There were little rust spots of dun-color against the blue of the hide that was like the blue of a late-afternoon Alberta sky. There was a star on his forehead.

"Horse," he said shakily, "your coat's the color of blue sky." He pulled the roan's head closer and something within him softened, then hardened with purpose.

"Sky, Sky," he whispered, trying the words on his lips. "That's what I'm going to call you." His voice stopped, then went on, filled with decision. "When I get you into the barn at Doctor Crane's and land that job!"

He lay down, staring into the dying fire.

He'd found himself now, and he knew that he had

found his horse. A sense of belonging to each other and of being alike filled him. Hadn't Luce found him on the doorstep? And hadn't he found the roan down here in the river bottom? They'd both been foundlings.

Glenn knew then that, above all else, he had to hold the faith of this outlaw and make him well. Together they would help each other.

But the roan's repeated anguished foot-waving told Glenn that the help he'd given him wasn't enough. If the roan were to live he would need real care—and soon.

He put out a hand to touch the foretop of the suffering outlaw. With his fingers entwined in the horse's hair, he lay staring into the firelight, impatiently waiting for dawn.

3. The Banana Split

AT DAYBREAK, Glenn rolled from beneath his Navajo blanket, his thoughts all on the roan. Pulling on his boots and his windbreaker, then putting on his hat, still wet from last night's soaking, he moved quickly down to the river to wash. The roan stood there, not far from where he had left him, miserably swinging his foot back and forth, back and forth.

For a moment, Glenn, as he came up, caught his breath and wondered if this horse would ever look like anything again. He was skin and bones. A chill dawn wind ruffled his blue-roan coat, showing spur scars along his lean belly, quirt welts along his jaws, and a jagged scar along his bony shoulder. But worst of all was the way he'd forgotten what had been done for him the night before and now looked evilly at Glenn, his ears back, his fever-laden eyes glaring.

Glenn knew he must save this horse. In some way this outlaw was part of his plan. Under his rough coat and in those eyes glazed with pain lay the makings of a horse that had to be kept alive. One who would be his companion and help him, taking the place of Roy H.

He walked up to the roan, laying a gentle hand on his rough hairy shoulder just above the scar. Something of the struggle that lay ahead communicated itself to them there, with the river rushing by, the sun lightening the eastern sky, and the chill wind blowing down from the Rockies. He started to talk to the roan then as he had always talked to Roy H.

The horse suddenly moved away, but the pain in his foot forced him to stop. He began to tremble, and put his muzzle down to touch this terrible hurt.

Glenn thought for a moment that he couldn't stand seeing how the roan suffered. A wave of compassion swept him, and his eyes caught the old jagged shoulder scar.

"Cougar claw you when you were a colt?" he asked softly. "And those spur scars," he went on, his voice shaking, "I'll bet you've been in a thousand rodeos."

The roan just stood, unable to move, his eyes alight with hatred for Glenn, whom he could only recognize as another rider to battle.

Glenn began once more to talk to him as he had been wont to talk with Roy H.

"Sky," he said. "That's your name, now. Sky, I'm going to cure you, fatten you up sleek. You'll be my horse and never hit a rodeo chute again." It was a promise.

Talking softly, he moved the few steps to his saddle, sacked it up, rolled the blanket and stuffed it in beside the saddle, then shouldered them both.

"I'll be back," he promised, taking a deep breath. "With the job all sewed up with Doctor Crane and with his ambulance to take you in."

The roan, beyond a slight movement of his ears, did not let on he'd heard.

Glenn, his belly tight with resolve, moved up the

riverbank and onto the graveled highway. He thumbed a ride with an oil truck into Cardston and, getting out just below the foot of the hill of the one-street town, moved to the sidewalk.

The *Old Chief Café*, laden with breakfast odors, stood right in front of Glenn.

He moved past it, the picture of the waiting horse hurrying him. Time enough to eat later, when he had his job nailed down and the roan in a stall with his foot cleansed and bandaged.

But just then Jim West, young, sleek, and dapper, his Uncle Walter Swanson's bank cashier, came riding up in a new Plymouth coupé.

"You're Glenn Barnes," he said, pulling to the curb and getting out. Crossing the few feet between them, he put a persuasive arm around Glenn's shoulder. He was that kind of a guy, always had to have a paw around you. "Glad to meet you, Glenn," he went on. "I'd have known you anywhere by Walt's description. He called me from Macleod yesterday and said to meet you here. He's staying over to buy the ranch."

"Buy the ranch? The *Shoestring?*" Glenn's heart sank. So that was why Uncle Walt hadn't wanted to take him. He'd wanted to have him out of the way to dicker with Abbie and Luce.

"Yes. He's bringing the old folks to Lethbridge. Goin' to give Luce a job as janitor at the bank. Now come on, Glenn. Let's have some breakfast. How about a stack of hot cakes and coffee? And a banana split to top it off? It's my favorite dish." Being careful of his pin-stripe gray suit, he disposed of Glenn's saddle and suitcase in the back of the coupé and propelled him through the café door and to a stool.

Glenn couldn't do more than perch there while his thoughts went round and round.

The roan's need kept shoving at him, and now mixed up with it was the fact that wily Uncle Walt was going to dicker Abbie and Luce out of the *Shoestring* and move them into Lethbridge.

Glenn felt pity for Abbie, and for Luce too. They would be lost in town. Imagine Luce a janitor! Imagine a man, used to the dignity and cleanness of the prairie, handling a mop.

Well, it was just one more reason to get that job with Doctor Crane, but quick.

"Listen, Mr. West—"

"Jim," the dapper round-faced chap beside him prompted. "We're Jim and Glenn now."

"Okay, Jim," Glenn said. "I'm not going to take Uncle Walt's bank job after all."

Jim West's astonishment showed on his round red face and in his baby-blue eyes.

"No?" he said. "You're going to pass up a chance to own a car like mine out there, and to see your folks settled in a nice little house on the edge of town?"

Glenn paused, wondering if he might be crazy. He thought of the roan, sick, and trusting him as he had shown last night; then of Abbie cooped up in a town house!

More than ever he felt he was right.

"Yes," he nodded. "I have other plans."

The hot cakes, crisp and brown, came. Jim made a ritual out of buttering them and creaming his steaming, fragrant coffee.

"Best hot cakes this side of Madison Square Garden," he said finally, around a huge bite. "Little restaurant off Times Square makes better ones." He winked at Myrtle Swing, the waitress, then swung back to Glenn. "We'll be seeing Madison Square Garden this winter, at the rodeo," he said. "We can take two weeks off. It's slack time then, and Walt likes to save the extra clerks' money. Gene Autry'll be there. Great guy, Gene is. Great friend of mine, mmuuph, f-f-ine boy," Jim tried to explain with his mouth full of hot cakes.

Glenn buttered his cakes without saying a word, then poured syrup over them. He poured cream in his coffee and all the time the picture of Sky's restless foot moved before his eyes.

"Eat hearty," Jim enthused. "Then we'll get along in that car of mine, bought with banking money."

Glenn, cutting his cakes, putting a bite in his mouth, tried to tell Jim that he had other plans.

But West was off on his own line.

"Walt told me about your losing your last eight dogies," he said. "But he has that all figured out. He's going to put up a new fence between the pasture land and the alfalfa meadow where the cows got too much green grass. That's after he gets Abbie and Luce off the place."

Glenn choked on his mouthful of cakes. A dull rage engulfed him.

The thought of Walt's trickery left him stunned.

He must hurry and get up to Doctor Crane's hospital with its cases of shiny instruments, the line of kennels with dogs being healed, and the barn in which Sky must find a stall in which to recover.

Jim finished his cakes and coffee and, with Glenn refusing one, a banana split. Then mistaking his silence for consent, he pushed Glenn toward the door.

He swept his money back into his hand.

"You pay in New York," he said, "after you've earned some at the bank. Here's two dollars, Myrt. Now come on, Glenn, let's go on up to the bank and to work."

He moved to the door and then out to the shiny coupé.

Glenn saw that if he wasn't to be kidnapped and taken bodily to Lethbridge, he'd have to start something. He hated to do this to Jim, too. The guy seemed okay. He was sincere in wanting to be friends and in wanting to help him get started at the bank.

But Uncle Walt's grasping scheme, and the roan's foot needing attention made him brush all this aside.

He paused a moment, watching Jim climb smugly behind the wheel of the car, then walked back to lift the trunk lid and retrieve his saddle and suitcase.

Putting them on the sidewalk, he straightened. The sun had come out, bright now. The hills in June lay green as Ireland, and the ribbon of water that was Lee's Creek laughed and riffled its way between its cottonwood-shaded banks beyond the main street.

It made him think of Roy H out there under the trees along the Old Man River, and of Sky and of his promise to bring him in.

Jim stuttered, "What—what is this, aren't you coming?"

Glenn told him then about his plans. He thanked him for driving down and tried to make him see why he had to go on alone.

Jim leaned out of the car, his eyes incredulous that

anyone could pass up a ready-made job and Walt's generosity.

"You mean," he said, a stunned look in his light-blue eyes, "you're passing up a lifetime cinch job at Walt's bank for thirty days with Doctor Crane?"

"Thirty days?" Glenn stuttered.

"Sure," Jim West's voice came with convincing sureness. "Ask anyone at the bank here in Cardston. I've talked to 'em. He's had four new assistants this year. No one ever lasts with Doc Crane. He's crazy-clean. He's a nut on sanitation. He'll can you for making the wind blow germs through his hospital."

Glenn eyed Jim West, while a kind of satisfaction filled him. Crane was the kind of man he wanted to work for. A man who would give him the right training. He'd need it before he finished the veterinarian courses and set up for himself.

"That's great," he said. "That's wonderful. I'll be cleaner than he is."

"Maybe," West said and leaned closer. "But it takes a pretty tough hombre to do the work Crane asks of his assistant." He rolled down the window and thrust his red face close to Glenn's, forgetting in his earnestness the way his fancy maroon tie pulled away from a spotless white collar. "You'll be up against Land Peters of the *Rolling R* in this fight about mange," he warned. "I suppose you know that. Peters doesn't like to dip his cattle, and he's got enough power around here to skip dipping them if he wants to. Crane hasn't the tact to handle Peters and he knows it. He'll be leaving it to you first thing you know."

Glenn shook his head. He hated to appear stubborn.

"I tell you, you won't last," Jim said. "The last man

rode right on out and over to Peters. The others lay down cold."

Glenn turned, his hands on his saddle. Making Alberta mange-free happened to be a hobby of his. It was right down the line of his own thinking.

"I'll try not to ride on out," he promised. In his perturbation, he pulled out his pocketknife and absently looked at it.

West spied the bits of blood.

So then, Glenn had to tell Jim about Sky.

Jim looked at him as though he were crazy—as though he'd ridden one bronc too many and it had made him foolish.

"You mean to say," he demanded, "that you think Crane'll let you take that outlaw into his barns?" Jim laughed, and held the car door open wide for Glenn to get in. "That settles it, dope." He grinned. "Hop in. Crane hates rodeos. He thinks they're cruel and a useless debasement of the horse that should be trained to be useful and not to pander to the pleasure-loving tastes of the public. 'Teach 'em tricks, sure,' he says. 'But don't make brutes of 'em. Don't make 'em killers.'"

Glenn smiled. He and Crane would get on, for that was the way he felt about horses too. Sky was proof of what rodeos did to a good horse.

"I've got to go now," he told Jim. "Got to go to Crane and get that job before somebody else lands it." He stopped. His voice soft. His eyes really filled with contrition for turning West down. "I'm sorry. Thanks for driving clear down here for me."

Jim shook his head. "Oh, I'll see you in Lethbridge yet. You know what'll happen?" He leaned close.

"Take this down under that Stetson of yours and see if it won't: Crane'll blow his top when he finds out about Sky, and out you'll go. Or else, and this will hurt worse, Crane'll give you the job. You'll heal the roan, get him fat and sassy, his coat shining, then the owner'll come and claim him. Or steal him away—"

"No," Glenn said. He stood waiting, wishing West would breeze off.

"Anyway you slice it," Jim said, "you'll wind up without a job and without the roan."

Glenn said softly, "I guess not, and thanks again, Jim," and turned to go.

"Last call," Jim said.

Glenn had to admit he'd been afraid Jim might overpower him with his arguments. But Jim was kicking over the smooth motor, and putting the car into gear.

Flinging the saddle to his shoulder, he picked up the yellow suitcase by the handle and swung up the sidewalk.

Jim followed alongside. "To show you my heart's in the right place, I'll run you up to Crane's hospital," he said, opening the door. "Hop in."

Glenn, after only a minute's pause, tossed his saddle once more into the trunk and, keeping hold of the suitcase, climbed in.

They drove up the hill and along the side street to stop before a small white building with a sign flapping over the door that read, A. R. CRANE, D.V.M.

Jim stopped the car and Glenn, his heart thudding, opened the door and got to the ground along with his stuff.

"So long, see you tomorrow, in Lethbridge." West

started his car, and then sped down the street and out of sight.

Glenn, his nerves taut, his mind on the roan and this job that he must get, turned. Shouldering his saddle and grasping the suitcase handle, he walked up the two steps and through the glistening white door.

4. Job Chaser

THE INSIDE of the waiting room was as Glenn had expected, but cleaner. Glistening with white paint, it fairly shone. The floor, laid with green and brown linoleum, had a new coat of glossy polish, in which Glenn might have seen his anxious face had he leaned over.

"No one can please Doc Crane," came West's remembered voice. "He's got a bug on cleanliness."

Glenn surveyed the walls and the rattan furniture covered with a crisp flower print.

"Just like I'll have some day," he whispered.

Through the door marked PRIVATE came a fox terrier's high shrill bark. Other dogs' voices, deeper in tone, chimed in.

A faint odor of carbolic acid filled Glenn's nostrils, making him tingle clean to his toes. A dull pounding ache for the job took possession of him, sending blood up through his neck to suffuse his face.

"Hello!" said a voice behind him.

Glenn swung to see a little girl of seven, with big, worried brown eyes, holding a basket in her lap. In the basket lay a sick cat. It had a white neck and Maltese markings.

Beside her stood a boy of perhaps twelve. He was

31

dressed in Levi's, a red bandanna around his neck, and he had two toy pistols strapped to his hips.

"Hello," Glenn said, instinctively moving toward the cat, dumping his stuff into a corner of the room.

"My kitty's sick," the girl said. "And Ricky Clements helped me bring him to the vet-er-in-ar-ian. Ricky's a law-and-order man. He's head of a club called The Range Riders. They've each got a horse and two guns apiece and they help keep law and order in the country."

In her pause for breath, Glenn picked up the sick kitten.

"Law and order," he said, rubbing the kitten's neck, feeling how hot its body was. "Maybe I can use you later on." He paused for a moment, remembering Jim West's warning about Peters, the grizzled old rancher, who owned two thousand head of cattle down on the Milk River toward the U.S. boundary line. "Maybe I can, Ricky. What does it take to get into your club?"

"Two guns and a horse to ride," the red-headed boy said without a smile. "You have to take an oath to stop crime and you have to know how to ride. 'Course you can ride. I saw you at the Calgary Stampede last year. You'd a'won the contest if that horse you drew had put up a fight."

Before Glenn could reply, the door marked PRIVATE opened and a girl's blonde head, above a white uniform, thrust through the door. She had lively blue eyes, a spot of glowing color in each cheek, and she walked impulsively into the room. He guessed she was around seventeen.

"Hello, Margie. Hello, Ricky." She turned toward Glenn who had been unable to move. Expecting Doc-

tor Crane, he was hardly prepared for this assured
girl.

"New assistant? I see you've taken hold already."
She laughed. "It's a good sign." It was evident to
Glenn that she liked his taking Margie's cat up for in-
spection.

Any other time Glenn would have grinned. Now,
he could feel the pressure of the roan's suffering upon
him.

"You think it is a good sign?" he managed. "I'm
Glenn Barnes from Macleod. And I want to be an
assistant here. I want the job."

"I guessed it," she said. "I'm Barbara Crane. And
I'd say you've got a good chance."

Glenn felt awkward before her assurance. His
hands felt huge as hay forks as he put Margie's kitten
gently back into the basket. How she could think he
might do was beyond him.

"I'm pretty awkward," he managed.

She brushed his remark aside, looking at him with
twinkling eyes that took in his neat clothes, his hair
parted and smoothly combed even though he'd slept
on his saddle.

"Dad will like you," she said. "And goodness knows
that will help. You see, he's had boys who didn't care,
and with all this trouble about Peters and the mange,
it was hard working with someone you didn't like, or
who didn't take an interest in the battle."

Glenn stared out of the window, watching a tumbleweed roll down the street. Goodness knows, he
cared, though he didn't see how anyone could tell it.
A kind of hope bubbled within him, listening to Barbara's encouraging words. He knew that Doctor

Crane had been sent out from Ontario to clean up the range. It would save the Dominion Government millions of dollars if it could be done. Glenn had been enthusiastic about the plan. Friends had kidded him. Everyone knew how he felt about animals. Maybe someone had said something to Doctor Crane—maybe it had been that friendly man he had driven with yesterday.

Glenn found his hands tight at his sides. He, too, believed that mange could be swept from the range. It was only laxness—not seeing that every cow was dipped twice, ten days apart, that had kept mange on the range so long. Laxness had allowed the skin disease to persist.

"I know," he said, surprised at the intensity of his voice. "I know about the struggle Doctor Crane is having and I believe I can help him to win. I want the job." He paused, not believing how easy it seemed to be.

Barbara stopped at the tone of his voice, then laughed.

"You won't be like Larry Parks, the last boy who had the job. He rode out to Peters' to inspect the dipping vat and didn't come back. Just threw in his lot with the *Rolling R*."

"No, I won't be like that," Glenn promised.

Suddenly Barbara's eyes widened. "I know you now. You're Luce and Abbie Barnes' boy, Glenn."

Barbara grew thoughtful for a moment. Two vertical lines formed between her eyes, then disappeared with her candid, "I think it's sweet, the way Luce Barnes helps boys by buying things, inventions and such." She stamped her foot. "You'll see. One day he'll make one of them pay off."

Glenn felt the same way about Luce and hearing Barbara say it made him feel more than ever that he'd land this job. He stood watching as Barbara walked to the window to stare out toward the east road.

"I wonder what's keeping Dad. He just went up to Daisy De Winton's ranch to inoculate some of her cows against t.b."

The clatter of barking dogs became sweet music to Glenn's ears.

"Boy, oh boy," he whispered to himself. "This is going to be a pushover."

Barbara's voice reached him.

"Perhaps while you're waiting," she said, "you'd like to see the place in which you're likely to work?"

Glenn, scarcely believing that he was here on the ground, nodded. "I'd like that," he said, and felt that he must be taken on here. He realized that he'd been telling himself that he would be but not really believing it.

Barbara turned to Margie.

"The doctor will be here any minute," she said softly. "He'll fix your kitty right away."

Glenn held the door for Barbara, then followed into the hospital proper. For a second he was conscious of a sense of belonging here. This was his world.

A fox terrier, white with one black ear, barked from one of the double row of kennels along the wall. Before them lay inlaid linoleum, spotless and polished.

In another kennel a red setter lay bandaged.

"Caught in a coyote trap. I think we'll save her leg," Barbara explained.

Turning to the left, she opened another door. "The operating room," she said.

Glenn's eyes moved in wonder to the case of surgical instruments, then on to the wall, to Doctor Crane's diploma. From Ames, Glenn read, where he intended going. Maybe he'd get the same room in Friley Hall that Doctor Crane had used.

He caught his breath in pleasure, his eyes moving back to the case of instruments. "Just like a doctor," he said.

Barbara stamped her foot. "Naturally," she exclaimed indignantly.

"I'm sorry," Glenn explained. "I meant to say that I was pleased."

"Of course," Barbara's frown smoothed out. "You see, Dad's touchy on that point. So many people look down on veterinarians, when they're really just as important as doctors. They protect children by inoculating cows agaist Bang's disease, which in humans is undulant fever. They save thousands of children from getting tuberculosis by seeing that the dairy herds are kept free of it."

She pointed to a huge X-ray machine. "For setting bones," she said. "And the fluoroscope, for studying fractures, finding foreign objects in intestinal tracts, among other things."

Glenn could only stand and stare, wishing that the doctor would come so he might get to work. He still could hope for his good fortune. As the door leading to the feeding room opened, and a rather slight, serious colored boy in immaculate white came through it, it became more clear to him that this doctor must be an all-right guy.

"This is Alan Roak," Barbara said. "He's been with

Dad for three years now. He's saving up money to go to the Ames College for Veterinarians."

Glenn's hopes soared as he shook the slender hand of Alan Roak. The doctor must be interested in boys planning to go to Ames.

"Hello, Alan," Glenn said.

Alan's greeting came, soft and friendly. With both courtesy and sincerity, he paid Glenn the compliment of making him welcome, even though he must have wondered about him after four other boys had come and gone.

"I hope Glenn's to take over where Larry Parks left off," Barbara explained.

Glenn knew that Alan's pause was not meant to discourage him. But it told him that the job was going to be no cinch. There would be days and nights of toil, riding in the hot summer and cold winter out on the range on emergency cases. You had to love animals.

Or was he wondering in that pause if Glenn would try to crowd him, want to take his position next to Doctor Crane? Maybe Larry Parks had pushed him around. He said, "Would you like to see the corrals? I'm just on my way there. That's where most of your work will be."

Glenn nodded eagerly.

"I'll run up to the house and make Dad a cup of coffee. He had to leave early and without much breakfast," Barbara said. Then she added, "Perhaps you'll come up too when he arrives. You can talk there."

Glenn hesitated.

It was obvious that Barbara thought he had the job nailed down. She seemed to brush away the fact, if she knew it, that he'd been a rodeo rider and that

Doctor Crane hated the whole idea of rodeos and what they did to horses.

Well, she should know her father.

"Yes," he said, "I'd like that, if I may. If your father wants me to."

"I'll see to that," Barbara said and walked off across the lot to the little white house with the green shutters, facing the opposite street.

Doctor Crane had two lots on two streets. Between them stretched the office building, the inside small-animal hospital and behind that the contagion ward, then the barns for outdoor patients.

Alan led the way through the corral gate and into the barn. Five stalls stretched down each side. In the first one a young bay filly stood in slings.

"She had a long illness: pneumonia. We had to sling her up," Alan explained. "I suppose you know that once a horse gets down it's the end of it."

Glenn nodded. He knew that all right.

The next two stalls were empty. The last stall on the left had a door leading outside. In it stood a small ambulance that could be hitched to a car. Probably the Dodge coupé he'd noticed in the garage just to the left of the corral.

"For Sky," Glenn whispered to himself, feeling an increased uneasiness and wishing the doctor would come.

Suddenly the faint purr of a car came to his ears. In spite of himself, Glenn stopped breathing. So much depended on this interview with Doctor Crane.

Alan said, "There's Doctor Crane now," and led Glenn across the lot and into the office.

Glenn was prepared to like the doctor on sight. But

the man who turned to him as Alan ushered him into the office puzzled him. Almost six feet two in height and with the quiet clipped voice of an eastern Canadian, he seemed efficient but cold. His eyes, deep gray and sunken in a thin long face, seemed hard to probe.

"Well, my lass?" he said, handling Margie's kitty. "Your cat has cat fever." At his motion Alan took the kitten, carried it into the treating room and laid it on a clean newspaper on the operating table. Doctor Crane prepared to give it a serum injection.

Taking a hypodermic needle from the sterilizer, he selected a bottle of serum from a row of bottles in the case, upended it, and emptied it of the brown liquid.

"You wait out in the other room, Margie," he said. "Law-and-Order, you may stay here if you like." With deft hands he injected the serum into the kitten's thigh as Margie disappeared through the door. "Now," he said, handing the kitten to Ricky Clements, "it's a question of feeding. The kitty's sick and won't eat, but you feed her warm milk with egg beaten into it every three hours and she'll be all right. Use a medicine dropper."

He turned to wash hands that Glenn noted were long and supple, then swung to Glenn.

For a moment their eyes met and held. Glenn could only see in this tall gaunt man the eyes of a doctor who had certain principles and would give no quarter. He thought of the man's bitter fight with Peters over mange, of the government's lax methods until Crane, fresh from Eastern practice, had come to throw down the gauntlet to Peters.

As he stared at Doctor Crane, he could scarcely believe that, a few moments ago, the winning of the job had appeared so easy.

"Well, young man," the doctor's voice reached Glenn. "What is it?"

Glenn hardly knew how to begin. He felt small and almost wished that he hadn't come. But the filly in the barn whinnied and brought back the memory of Sky down there in the river bottom, sick enough to die.

"I'm Glenn Barnes," he managed. "I—I've come for a job as your assistant."

Doctor Crane looked at him. His eyes strayed out through the door to Glenn's saddle.

"Any experience?" he asked, drying his hands with meticulous care.

Glenn gulped.

"No," he said. "None beyond working on a ranch." Honesty compelled him, because he wanted the job to be rock solid, to say, "Except around a ranch and as a rodeo rider."

"Oh! You like to ride in rodeos? Like what it does to horses?"

"No, sir," Glenn said, feeling his chances slipping, yet fighting for them. "But I had to have money for the ranch. It was on its last legs." He paused.

Doctor Crane's cool gray eyes measured him. "And you made enough to save it?"

"No, sir, the last cows died of bloat." Glenn swallowed hard. "Then my horse, Ray H, died of colic and —" he dived clean off the board into the waters of the future. "I've got to earn money to give to Luce and Abbie and to go to Ames College."

Doctor Crane sat down heavily in a chair and brushed his hair from discouraged eyes. He stared out of the window to the rolling hills beyond town, without seeming to see them. It was evident to Glenn that he had little faith in taking on another assistant.

"Here she goes," Glenn couldn't help whispering deep within himself.

"You know about Parks?" the doctor asked. "And how hard the work is here? Riding the vats, bucking the ranchers' opposition to dipping?"

Glenn couldn't answer before Barbara came out of the house and through the door to them. Was it only a few minutes ago that she had left and things had looked so rosy? He guessed so, but that had been time enough for everything to change plenty.

"I've made some coffee, Dad," she said. "You can drink it while you're talking to Glenn."

"Oh." Doctor Crane stood up. His voice held a note of reserve. "That will taste good. Come along, Barnes. Barnes?" He stopped. "The name's familiar."

Before Glenn could reply, Barbara said, "Glenn Barnes is from Macleod."

"Barnes from Macleod?" Doctor Crane's eyes looked intently at Glenn's taut face while his mind searched the past, then came up with the answer. "Adopted son of Lucifer and Abbie Barnes?" he asked, frowning.

Glenn knew that Doctor Crane was thinking he had picked a maverick for sure if he gave him a job. What good would a boy be who had grown up around old Luce Barnes who had blown a ranch for a lot of useless inventions?

But something stiffened within Glenn like a wet

Manila lariat. Luce was swell. He could spend ten ranches for a sea-water machine if he wanted to. Hadn't he taken him off a doorstep and shielded and loved him in his own way for eighteen years?

Glenn straightened and gave Doctor Crane back look for look.

"Yes, sir," he said proudly. "Luce and Abbie Barnes' adopted son. That's right."

"I see," Doctor Crane said, his tone doubtful.

Glenn could fancy his job petering out like dogies drifting from a tenderfoot hazed herd. But flat honesty, clear as the sun on slab rock, made him come all the way. It must have been the kind of desperation Sky'd had facing the blizzard he'd been born into.

"I've got to tell you," he said, with Doctor Crane's eyes upon him. "Before you decide about me, I've got a horse."

The corners of Doctor Crane's thin mouth twitched.

"Most boys have," he said. "You could ride him on your inspection trips if you wished."

"You don't understand," Glenn explained, a dull feeling inside him. "This is a rodeo outlaw. He's been beaten up and is sick with an infected foot. He's a castoff down along St. Mary's River and about to cash in."

Doctor Crane's eyes narrowed.

"An outlaw! A rodeo killer, and you want to bring him here. You'd want me to treat him. You'd want the ambulance to bring him in?"

Glenn could see no other way. "That's right, sir," he said. "It's urgent."

Glenn stood, hardly daring to breathe, in the silence

that fell. The fox terrier's barking sounded like chattering.

Doctor Crane turned to him then. "I can overlook Luce," he said. "You can have the job if you forget this outlaw."

"Forget Sky?" Glenn blurted.

"Sky?" Doctor Crane's eyebrows raised.

"The outlaw. It's the only name that would fit his blue coat," Glenn explained.

"Humpf!"

Glenn steadied himself by the table. He couldn't believe that Doctor Crane would hinge the job on Sky. A sickness filled him.

"Well, young man?" Doctor Crane demanded.

The smell of the hospital came tantalizingly to Glenn once more. The wonderful feel of the place that was so much what he wanted. Alan Roak's soft voice drifted through the door, close and cozy, as he moved the dogs out to their runs for the morning feed and water.

But then the picture of the roan crowded all else out. Sky was sick and a part of himself. Sky trusted him.

"I—I can't give up Sky," Glenn blurted, then watched in concern the way Doctor Crane's eyes narrowed and his long veined hands clasped the arms of his chair.

"As you wish," the doctor said stiffly and turned away. "Good-bye, Mr. Barnes."

Saying good-bye to Barbara and to the doctor carefully, so that he wouldn't show the tumult within him, Glenn still couldn't take in the fact that he'd missed the job.

But it must be so. He stood out on the porch now, with his suitcase in his hand and his saddle across his shoulders.

There was no place to go but back to town to flag a ride to Sky. And there was Doctor Crane's sign squeaking out a doleful "so long."

With slow dogged steps Glenn moved down the street to the main artery leading toward the river bridge.

A red truck came by.

Glenn flagged it down.

"Goin' to Lethbridge?" a burly voice asked, and the cab door opened.

Glenn clambered in, the picture of the last few hours teasing him as he slammed the door and felt the truck move on. He couldn't figure it. He'd thought he had the job. It had been so close and wonderful. He had almost lived it for a few happy moments.

"Just to the river bridge," he said, hardly believing his own voice. "I have a sick horse down there."

The truck picked up speed and in a few moments slowed to a stop at the bridge. Glenn got out, dragging his stuff, his eyes already searching the river bottom.

"Thanks a lot," he said.

"Okay, buddy."

The truck moved on.

Glenn raked the length of the river area with anxious eyes. There was the camp site of last night, the dead embers of the fire and beyond, the racing river.

Panic gripped Glenn.

Sky was nowhere in sight.

5. The Lost Roan

GLENN moved down the bank, carrying his saddle and suitcase with him. Maybe the roan was down in the water. Sometimes a horse fell and drowned trying to get a drink to assuage the fever raging within him. He reached the flat and moved toward his old camp site.

A chicken hawk fled from the high branches of a cottonwood. A covey of Hungarian partridge, brown and fast as bullets, fled along the riverbank, then with a wide curve flew up and out of sight across the flat prairie.

Glenn kept thinking of the star on the roan's forehead that was so much like the one Roy H'd had.

He swallowed and felt a wave of faintness creep over him. "Take it easy," he whispered and reached the dead ashes.

There was no roan. No sight of him met Glenn's searching eyes. There was nothing but the cold embers of the fire and the flat mashed-down place among the weeds where Sky had lain.

Glenn gulped and felt then that he should never have left the horse.

After a moment, he bent to unsack his saddle

enough to get his lariat. Straightening, he began a wide circling of the flat lands along the river.

But there was still no sign of the roan.

At a bend in the river he paused. "He couldn't have gone any farther than this. Not on three legs."

He stood staring at the swirling water flowing past. He moved along the bank, his heart beating fast, his eyes scanning each eddying pool as he passed.

It wasn't until he had gone past the camping place and on up the river a hundred yards that he found a trace of the horse.

"Here's his track," Glenn whispered, staring down at three hoofmarks and the blur of a fourth. "Get goin'," he breathed and followed the track to the water's edge, where a big eddying pool cut under the bank in a deep swirling current of roily water.

At first it seemed as though there was no horse there. But suddenly, almost at Glenn's feet, came a faint nicker. He looked down and there, right at the edge of the bank, swimming to keep afloat, his head drenched, his eyes glazed with fever, was Sky.

For a moment Glenn could not move.

"He's done for," swept through his mind. "He won't fight."

Glenn thrust the thought aside. With swift sure hands he uncoiled his lariat and tossed the rope toward the drowning horse's head.

But Sky, schooled by the rake of spurs along his flanks, the whir of the cutting quirt along his neck, thought all men enemies. He had forgotten Glenn's gentle aid. Laying back his ears, he dodged his head from the loop and slipped downstream and out into the eddying current.

Glenn pitched after him, sobbing in his throat.

"He'll drown!" he cried. "Drown right here in the river."

And it seemed as though the roan horse would drown. His head went under. His muscled, scarred body whirled over in the water and disappeared from sight.

Throwing off his windbreaker and grasping his lariat in his hand, Glenn plunged wildly into the river. With powerful strokes he swam toward the place where the roan had sunk from sight.

The horse would have to surface sometime.

Then suddenly, right at Glenn's side, the roan split the surface of the water. Coming up with a surge, breathing air into his tortured lungs, he showered Glenn with water.

Glenn dog paddled.

"Sky, Sky," he pleaded. "Let's get out of here."

Sky turned on him, ears back, head thrust forward. With a rush of his body he lunged over Glenn, forcing him beneath the water.

Fighting free of the roan's body, Glenn surfaced. The roan again plowed over him.

Glenn's wind failed. His mouth filled with water that rushed down into his lungs. A buzzing filled his head.

He fought to the surface once more.

Sky was there, attacking, pushing him down and under.

The past filled Glenn's drowning mind. Roy H, Abbie and Luce, and even the roan.

Glenn gave up. He knew that he was through. But if only he could try one last time; make one more effort to come to the surface and save Sky. With feeble arms, he pushed his way to the river surface.

The roan again!

But suddenly a voice came from the bank. A familiar voice, that of Doctor Crane, and behind him a swift flash of the ambulance and Law-and-Order.

Again Glenn found himself thrust under.

But a courage filled him. It lent strength to his arms. The doctor was a good guy after all. There would be a chance for Sky to recover, and beyond that a job for Glenn as assistant—Ames, and maybe his name on that shingle with Doctor Crane's.

With his last strength, Glenn forced his body to the surface, took a deep breath, rolled from the roan's path and struck out for the bank.

"Give me the rope," Doctor Crane said, dragging Glenn up the bank. "Give it to an old chump."

"No, I'll take it," Glenn said. Fighting for wind, he coiled the stiff Manila rope and, with a fling, sent it over the roan's head and jerked it taut.

"Wonderful!" Doctor Crane said. "Now, we'll pull him to shore, and I'll tell you that you're hired."

The two men, with Law-and-Order lending a hand, pulled the roan to the edge of the water.

"Let him get his breath," Crane said. Then he turned to Glenn. "You know, I had a sick horse when I was a boy. It started me on the road to Ames. I'd forgotten it until you left the office. I'm sorry."

Glenn could scarcely believe that the doctor stood here, and the ambulance, which must have been skillfully threaded down the bank and through the trees to the river's edge. It had all been something like a roller coaster, getting this job. West's saying he wouldn't, Barbara so sure he would, Doctor Crane's brushing him off and now, right here, putting it in the bag.

Warmth filled Glenn and thankfulness, and an urge to get Sky moving toward the hospital. "Skip it," he said, with a grin, "I was young once myself."

In the laugh that followed, they got the roan to hobble to the dry ground. Sky stood, weaving with weakness, his right foot upheld.

Glenn looked the horse over critically, seeing his strong short-coupled back, the small head, the slender powerful legs, and firm well-knit body. Again, as it had last night, came the feeling that the blue's future was his future; that they were all tied up together.

But that foot?

Doctor Crane took one look at it, and said, "There's no time to lose. We'll have to get him to a stall at once."

Glenn took hold of the rope and tried to lead Sky toward the ambulance, while Ricky, from behind, tried to shoo him with a willow branch.

"No, don't do that," Doctor Crane said. "Never hit a horse or scare him into doing anything. They are nervous. They take on the mood of the master and do things for him from kindness."

Suddenly, as Sky came at the doctor on three feet, the doctor stepped nimbly aside.

"Like that?" Ricky laughed.

Doctor Crane smiled, and Glenn thought, he's certainly human after all.

They got the roan to the ambulance. Glenn let the ramp down, but Sky balked at walking up the cleated incline.

"Let's do it this way," Glenn said. Taking the end of the lariat he passed it through the front slat of the trailer, then brought it around Sky's rump. "Now, all together."

The three pulled, forcing Sky up the ramp and inside. Once there, he seemed to grow weaker and, as the ramp closed behind him, sank to the floor trembling.

"He's having a chill," Doctor Crane said. "He's a sick horse."

Glenn made no answer. He could only think of getting Sky to the hospital barn.

As Doctor Crane climbed into the Dodge and, with Ricky beside him, started the engine, Glenn piled horse blankets on the shaking roan.

"I'll drive as fast as I can," Doctor Crane called.

Glenn, beside Sky, nodded, leaning into the motion of the starting ambulance.

It climbed out of the river bottom to the prairie, weaved along the grass to the road and, hitting gravel, ran swiftly back to town and into the hospital yard.

They pulled into the barn runway, and Glenn got out to let down the ramp, as Doctor Crane came up.

Glenn's eyes met those of the doctor, swung to the trembling roan, then came back to the veterinarian once more.

"Do you think you can save him?" he whispered.

Doctor Crane paused, then, with a slow look at Sky, turned grave eyes to Glenn.

"If I do, it will be a miracle," he said.

6. Magic World

GLENN turned and made ready to lift the horse from the ambulance with the derrick. Sky's recovery seemed all tied in with this magic world of healing that he had entered.

Letting down the ramp, he said, "Guess he'll never make it under his own steam. We'll have to hoist him into the stall."

Doctor Crane, brusque again, nodded, then moved toward the barn door.

"I'll get my instruments and send Alan out to help," he said. It seemed that he'd suddenly begun to regret entering into this plan.

Glenn nodded, wondering, then moved in beside Sky.

Alan, slight and quiet, came grudgingly through the barn door.

It was natural, Glenn decided, for Alan to be a little suspicious. Here was a new assistant coming on. He might be no good, or he might be good enough to take first place with the doctor.

"Sorry to be so much trouble," Glenn began.

Alan waved his hand, then scowled. "Don't you know we'll have to work the bands under his belly?"

he demanded. "It's the only way we can hoist him up and run him along the track to his stall."

Glenn took the bands Alan handed him.

"Okay, Sky," he said, bending down to whisper into the roan's ear. "We'll sling you up in a jiffy."

Sky did not move. He lay with his head limp on the bedding of the trailer, his eyes closed and his breath coming sharply. Glenn thrust the bands under his side.

"Don't you know we'll have to turn him on his side?" Alan groused, coming in to help. "Then we roll him back so we can get the bands under him to connect with the pulley hook."

Together, they rolled the sick horse on his side, slipped the web bands under, then rolled him back.

"Okay, now connect the rings in these belts with the pulley hook," Alan snapped.

Glenn couldn't help noticing how resentful the boy seemed. He sensed that things weren't going to be too easy here.

"All right, Alan," he agreed. "Here goes." Adjusting the four ends with the rings through the hook, he grasped the pulley chain along with Alan, and together they began slowly hoisting Sky to his pins.

"Easy," Glenn cautioned, standing close to the horse. "Okay, Sky," he said. "We must get you into your stall."

The chain rattled through the pulleys, tightening on the hooks; the web under the roan tightened slowly, easily lifting him to his feet.

"Now, run the ambulance out from under him," Alan ordered, as the roan's feet left the ambulance floor.

Glenn, with a quick glance at Alan's face, slipped into the Dodge seat and, starting the motor, ran the car ahead its length.

"Okay, now to let him down," Alan said. Slipping the chain through the pulleys, he dropped the roan so that his three good feet touched the plank floor. "Now, into the stall. And take him easy."

Glenn grasped Sky's body, and together the two boys pushed the roan along the runway to a division in the track, then into the third stall on the left. In the fourth stood a sleepy buckskin gelding. The horse, Glenn sensed glumly, that he would probably ride on his range inspection trips, if he lasted here long enough to make one. Glenn thrust the thought from him and turned back to Sky.

Sweet mountain hay lay in the iron feed rack. Bright golden straw lay underfoot. Within a neck's length, clear water ran through a porcelain bowl.

"There you are," Glenn said, touching Sky's neck. "Home at last." The words had a hollow sound to him, with Alan's unexpected glowering and Doctor Crane's sudden shift of mood.

Buck, in the next stall, opened his eyes, nickering softly, then chewed lazily on a timothy stalk that stuck from his muzzle.

Sky did not open his eyes, but stood quietly sagging on the web bands, his right forefoot moving uneasily back and forth, back and forth.

Glenn swung, wondering where Doctor Crane was, just as the tall gaunt doctor came through the barn door. A flood of gratitude filled Glenn. Watching the doctor take Sky's pulse, then run his hand down to lift his injured forefoot, he vowed he'd work his head off to stick here.

But his heart sank at the doctor's grim stare at Sky's rowel-marked sides, the quirt scars along his jaws and the way Crane flinched away from Sky who stiffened at his touch.

"An old outlaw who'll never, never be any good," he grumbled. Then he bent to examine the foot.

Glenn thought otherwise, but kept discreetly silent.

"You dug this out?" the doctor's eyes rose.

Glenn, expecting he'd done the wrong thing, nodded. "I'm sorry. I had only a pocketknife and the light of a campfire."

"A good job, and possibly saved his life, worse luck for him. The roan will probably find his way back into the arena," the doctor said. "What did you find in it?"

"A piece of granite," Glenn watched the doctor's face for some sign of relenting. "It was imbedded in the frog."

"A thrush," Doctor Crane said, bending once more to the foot. "Hard to cure and often leaves the foot disfigured. I'll have to go a little deeper to get bottom drainage."

Glenn, watching the doctor get his farrier's knife and once more pick up Sky's foot, couldn't help but think of his words: "The roan will probably find his way back into the arena."

"Never," Glenn breathed. He grew silent and thrilled watching Doctor Crane's deft hands probing the wound, bringing out bits of gravel, then paring down the wound till it bled clean blood.

"Wonderful," Glenn whispered to himself. "I don't blame him for being short. He's seen a lot of horses and a great many poor assistants." He drew a deep breath, watching Doctor Crane wash out the wound with Lysol water brought by Alan, then skillfully pack the wound with sulpha.

In ten minutes the roan was as comfortable as his foot would allow for the time being.

Glenn watched the doctor straighten from his work, and waited for some sign of his relenting.

The doctor turned to Alan.

"Clean up, sterilize the instruments," he said, then moved to go.

"Nothing, not a word," Glenn whispered, downing his disappointment. "He's busy, that's all; pushed to the limit and fed up with assistants who don't come through."

The doctor, almost as an afterthought, turned to touch Glenn's drenched clothes.

"You're wet," he said. "You'd better go up to the house and change." His manner said, "With all there is to do around here, we don't want you sick as well as the outlaw."

Glenn mustered a "Thanks, Doctor, I'll get my stuff from your ambulance." Going by him, Glenn couldn't help saying to Alan in an aside, "Kind of sharp, isn't he?"

"You would be, too," Alan snapped back, "if you had this problem of cleaning up the mange around southern Alberta. Especially with Land Peters, the powerful rancher, to buck you."

Glenn took his suitcase and saddle from the ambulance.

"When Barbara shows you to your room," Doctor Crane said as he was leaving, "change your clothes, then go to the hospital. Alan will show you what to do to help." The doctor moved toward the barn door, then turned again. "As for your outlaw, soak the foot in hot Lysol water three times a day and keep it packed in sulphanilamide between treatments. We'll keep him in a sling, for if he gets down he'll give up."

The doctor turned once more to go but still did not. He swung instead to study Glenn.

A maroon station wagon drew up in front of the hospital and a small blonde woman in a big floppy hat and gay print dress got out to step daintily up the walk and in through the hospital's front door.

Deep sounds of annoyance broke from Doctor Crane's throat as he paused in the barn doorway. His eyes grew dark with impatience, watching her.

"Drat that Daisy De Winton, what's wrong at her ranch now?" With long steps he covered the ground to the back door of the hospital and disappeared.

"She's the boss and owner of a purebred Hereford ranch up Lee's Creek," Alan explained in answer to Glenn's look. "Doctor calls the place *Confusion* ranch, which is wrong because it's in good order under Daisy. The confusion comes in when the doctor tries to dodge Daisy." Alan, picking up after the doctor, added with a rare smile, "She's rich and she wants to take Doctor Crane out of all this."

Glenn had already lost interest in Daisy De Winton. She might have been a Ubangi with a dish in her lower lip for all he cared. He wanted Sky well for inspection trips over sunny hills. It would be great to have Sky's big powerful body under him. He'd win his confidence and teach him tricks.

Suddenly a thought, sharp as a knife thrust, came to him. What if Sky lost his hoof, or it was misshapen, making him a cripple?

Glenn took hold of the stall planks, feeling his knees buckle. But suddenly, as he looked at Sky, at that scarred body, the bitten neck and frosted ears, a vision of the colt's birth came to him. Probably foaled in a snowbank with the wind howling and the mare trying to shield him from a prowling wolf.

Iron filled Glenn. It straightened him.

"Sky," he whispered, coming close and laying a hand on the roan's hot body. "We'll stick it out here. You'll get well, and I'll make the grade with the doctor. I don't care how abrupt he is. We'll go places."

He turned then, and, dumping his saddle from the sack, hung it on a peg in the little tack room at the front of the barn. Then picking up his suitcase he moved through the corral and across the lot to Doctor Crane's house.

Barbara, eyeing his wet figure and chattering teeth as he stood on the kitchen doorstep, let him in.

"Been swimming?" she asked, with a laugh that trailed off as she met his eyes. "I'm sorry," she said, "your room's this way."

She led him through the big white kitchen to a room opening off it on the left. Beyond lay a bathroom, and the sitting room through another door on the opposite side of a hall.

"This is your room," she said, opening a door. "It was Larry Parks' too."

Glenn, walking across the threshold, remembered

that Larry Parks had ridden out from under the doctor's job. Staring at the popcornlike bedspread and the braided rug, and the sampler with *God Bless Our Home* framed on the wall, he knew he wanted to stay here until he'd made enough for Ames. He wished Barbara would go.

"Fine," he said. "But I've got to change."

"I'll make you some hot chocolate," Barbara said generously, lingering in the doorway.

Glenn could see that Barbara did everything on impulse. She was as open as a summer pass through the mountains. Anything she said sprang from her generosity and love of talk.

She said now, "You'll make the grade here all right, don't worry. It's just that Dad's worried about Peters and working too hard."

Glenn wished he could believe that, but more, he wished she'd drift.

"Alan's working hard to get on to veterinarian school too," she explained. "He wants to marry Doris, who works in a drug store in New Orleans. Naturally he's suspicious of you coming in here. Not that there's any reason for it. But he lost out so often before he came here. Then, he senses that he's not really wise to the range side of this job and he's sensitive on that score too."

"Maybe so," he said, trying to hide his impatience.

"And he's very sensitive about his accordion playing. He's wonderful on it. But do you suppose he'll play down at my young people's church group? No." She laughed ruefully. "He's afraid they'll say he's just a comic—"

Glenn felt the press of Doctor Crane's manner and his suggestion that he come to the hospital, pronto.

"Scram," he said to Barbara. "I've got things to do at the hospital."

With the slam of the door and Barbara's light laugh going down the hall, Glenn raced out of his wet clothes and into the dry ones he fished from his suitcase. He slipped into a blue shirt, pulling it over his shock of rust-red hair, put on clean socks Abbie had knit, pausing for a second, with one sock half on to wonder about Walt and Luce and Abbie and the deal for the *Shoestring*.

Should he try to interfere?

Glenn decided not to, smiling softly, and taking heart when he thought of Abbie in her house.

"It would be one thing for Luce to sell the *Shoestring* land. But when Uncle Walt came to moving Abbie from the inside of her kitchen, well—" Glenn's smile widened. "That would be something to see!" Tonight he'd write her saying he had landed a job with a veterinarian.

Slipping into his windbreaker, he moved out of the door.

Barbara met him at the kitchen door.

He would have slipped by, but she stopped him, thrusting the cup of steaming chocolate into his hand.

"Drink it," she ordered, with a laugh.

Glenn gulped the drink with one eye on the hospital door he could see through the kitchen window.

"Okay, I'm off," he said, handing her the empty cup, and moving toward the door.

"I'll be out later to supervise," Barbara called after him.

"I'll bet," Glenn called back, wishing Alan and Doctor Crane were half as friendly.

He sped through the door, across the lot, and into the back door of the hospital.

The terrier with the black ear still barked incessantly. The silky hunter lay quietly in her iron-grill kennel, her brown eyes deep with pain, but silent about it.

"Over here," Alan called through the door leading to the washing room.

Glenn moved in beside him, anxious to please.

"We're late with the morning's routine," Alan said shortly.

Because of the roan, Glenn told himself.

"But we'll make up for it now." Alan motioned to the empty kennels. "I've put the dogs out; now clean the kennels."

Quietly, he showed Glenn how to take the two newspapers from the kennel floors.

"Scrub 'em out now with hot Q.A. solution," he ordered. "Hose 'em down; then mop the floor with purex solution."

Throughout the day Glenn worked under Alan's impatient guidance, cleaning the double row of kennels, bringing in the dogs from their runs, tending the filly in the first stall of the barn.

In the evening, after a dinner at which Doctor Crane barely spoke, Glenn walked through the twilight to the rear door of the hospital. His arms ached from scrubbing the hospital floor. His head buzzed with the constant remembrance of Alan's short muffled commands.

"Chalk up one lost day for me and a win for Alan and the doctor," he told himself.

Alan came to the door of his little rear-room apartment, where he slept and usually ate because he took the night duty. Behind him on the desk, Glenn saw as he paused, loomed a picture of a small slender girl.

Doris, his girl friend, Glenn decided. And she's nice. I don't blame Alan for wanting to make sure of his job here.

Glenn thought that the roan might pull Alan out of his shell. If they were working on the foot and he was interested, he might even talk to him about Doris.

But all Alan said was, "Get a bucket, fill it with hot water, add Lysol according to the directions on the bottle. Soak the outlaw's foot in it for half an hour; then I'll help you pack it in sulpha."

"I thought sulpha drugs were only for humans," Glenn said, turning toward the treatment room and the shelf of bottles.

"Hardly," Alan said, dryly. "They're doing things in medicine for animals now. Veticillin for infections, an improved tuberculin for protecting dairy cows from tuberculosis."

Glenn thought Alan might go on, but suddenly, as quickly as he had started talking, Alan broke off.

"Get the Lysol," he snapped.

Glenn got the Lysol and water and walked alone out through the dark corral and into the barn. Alan hadn't come along as he'd hoped he would.

Snapping on the light, Glenn moved toward the roan's stall.

Buck opened his eyes, nickering sleepily, but Sky did not move. He just stood, letting his weight sag in the sling, and moved his foot ceaselessly back and forth.

Glenn moved quickly into the stall, trying to keep from noticing how Sky's ribs showed through his hide. Bending down, he stripped off the blood-soaked bandages and put the feverish leg deep in the antiseptic water.

"Easy, boy," he whispered. "Easy, and let's see what this will do."

A quietness settled over the barn. No sound came but the fever-driven breathing of Sky as Glenn laved the hot foot with his hands.

Glenn sat working mechanically, letting his eyes go around the rafters of the barn, shadowy and dark as his thoughts. He hadn't made a dent in Alan the whole day, and Doctor Crane might just as well have said right out, "Why did I ever let myself in for this boy and an outlaw horse?"

Suddenly, there was Alan leaning on the side of the stall and staring down at Glenn.

"Okay, it's soaked enough," he snapped. "Let's bandage the foot."

Glenn nodded and bent to help Alan, taking the bucket away and helping with the packs.

Perhaps tomorrow would be different, he decided, squaring his shoulders. He would have to work harder, that was all. Alan wasn't to blame nor Doctor Crane. They both had their troubles.

Glenn's eyes moved back through the shadows to study the roan sagging in his sling. "How's he doing, Alan?" he asked hopefully.

In silence, Alan felt along Sky's underjaw.

"His pulse is faster," he said, at length, then

gathered up the used bandages. "Anyway, what's it matter?" he asked bluntly, staring at the sprawled *C* brand on the roan's thigh. "If he got well, you'd just sleek him up for his real owner to come along and claim him, wouldn't you? He's probably Balleau's. Balleau is just the kind to do this to an animal and then turn it loose to die. He doesn't dare show his face around Alberta, but make it worth his while and he'll not ask, he'll just take. He can't get a powerful fighter like this roan every day."

With that Alan turned to walk to the barn door.

"You'll have to ask the doctor how the horse is," he said, then turned, to disappear into the darkness.

Glenn watched Alan out of sight, then he turned to Sky, to run a hand along the roan's neck. The horse seemed more feverish. Glenn's breath caught. If he should lose Sky now. Or if the horse got well and then the owner came along? And how was he really? Should he ask Doctor Crane?

But suddenly Glenn knew that he couldn't bother Doctor Crane. The doctor thought of Sky as just an outlaw.

No, Glenn shook his head. He'd have to play it his way, and fight it through, waiting for the doctor to suggest and advise.

With his heart heavy he sat down and wrote to Abbie and Luce, *I've landed a job with Doctor Crane. He's wonderful.* Then he told them about the hospital and about Alan and Sky.

This done, he whispered in the darkness, "Tomorrow the doctor will tell me how Sky really is."

But in the morning and in the days to follow, Glenn got little satisfaction from Doctor Crane about Sky.

The doctor was scrupulous in his care of the roan's foot, examining it and advising treatment. But he never came out of his shell, or treated the horse as anything but "an outcast who might live or die, what did it matter?"

Going the rounds: letting the dogs out into the runs, feeding, scrubbing, breaking eggs into milk, measuring out drops of cod liver oil for milk, Glenn felt that he wasn't really needed here.

Everything seemed so quiet, so impersonal. As though everyone was just waiting for him to make a mistake and throw up the sponge.

7. First Assignment

GLENN worked on hopelessly for two weeks. Then one windy day in June, as he paused beside the red setter's kennel, he heard Doctor Crane's curt busy voice on the telephone in his office.

Wondering what could make the doctor's voice sound so concerned, Glenn put his hand in to stroke the setter's head. The doctor had saved her leg, but she was still far from well. She lay now, her brown eyes fixed on the door through which she knew her master, Lieutenant Commander Harmon of the *Double Anchor* ranch, would come. He would take her back to the hills filled with delicious scents of Hungarian partridge and prairie chicken, and the quack of the wild ducks on hidden lakes.

Suddenly Doctor Crane came out of the office. He pulled impatiently at his white coat and his face warned the boy.

"Glenn," he said, two vertical lines between his gray eyes. "I'm swamped with work here, an operation on a hound, and just now Peters called and wants fifty calves vaccinated today against blackleg."

Glenn stood with the bowl of milk and eggs he had been fixing for the yippy fox terrier in his left hand. So this was it, his first assignment, and with Land

Peters who owned two thousand head of cattle on the Milk River just on the Canadian side of the border.

That it was a test, Glenn sensed instantly. A sort of buzzing started in his head, and his mouth went dry. "Yes, sir, Doctor Crane," he said, poking the milk and eggs into the terrier's cage.

"Come into the treating room," the doctor said. "I'll give you the serum and the hypodermic needle with instructions."

Quietly Glenn followed the tall doctor.

A dog lay strapped to the table in the treating room, a deep slash wound along his shoulder.

Alan, an ether cone in his hand, held it over the dog's nose. He did not glance up as Glenn came in.

"Wolf attack," the doctor explained. "One of Peters' best wolfhounds, he's condescended to have me treat."

Glenn felt the antagonism toward the rancher in Doctor Crane's voice. It didn't sound right to him. Probably it put Peters' back up. There should be some other way to proceed if he was ever to win Peters over. He kept silent. Funny that Peters wanted his calves treated for blackleg the very day he knew Crane was busy with his dog.

Doctor Crane pulled a bottle of dark fluid from the refrigerator and handed it to Glenn. From a case of surgical supplies he selected a gleaming chromium hypodermic barrel and three sturdy needles in a wooden cylinder. From a shelf of medicines he took a small bottle of alcohol.

"Sterilize the needle in this," he ordered. "Then use 5 cc's from this bottle. Inject it in the shoulder muscle of each calf."

With a quick glance at the wolfhound now well under the ether, he added, "Take Buck. Store your stuff in the saddle bags." Stepping to the dog, he turned up the eyelids. He murmured, "Not quite ready." He went back to Glenn.

"You have vaccinated for blackleg before?" he asked.

Glenn had done the vaccinating on the *Shoestring* for years. He nodded, and turned to go.

"Oh, yes," the doctor tossed a bombshell. "You might ride through Peters' cattle on the way home and look for signs of mange."

Glenn caught his breath. This would be something, to give a look through Peters' herd. It would be like riding through an atomic plant looking for a particular bomb.

"Yes, sir," he said. "I'll examine as many as I can."

"You'd recognize mange if you saw it?" Doctor Crane's eyes met his sharply.

Glenn did not smile. A lifetime with cattle and the prevalence of mange on the reserve and through the West had taught him all there was to know about spotting the rough hair, the welts imbedded by the tiny spiderlike insect causing mange. These welts were what made two dippings, seven days apart, necessary. The first dipping killed the hatched larvae. The second dipping killed those that hatched seven days later.

It was this feature of the disease that made it so hard to stamp out. The first dipping was fine, but the second was a nuisance, and a few cattle, missed on this second dipping, kept the disease alive and ready to spread another year.

Glenn knew all of this.

He said soberly, feeling his responsibility and the fact that the doctor was piling it on, "Yes, sir. I think I do, sir."

In the moments that followed, Glenn got some slight insight into Doctor Crane. The man was wonderful. Look at the deft way he threaded a surgical needle with gut for the operation on the hound. The caution he used, pinching the dog between the toes to make sure he was "out" before proceeding.

He explained this to Glenn, seeming to want to be friendly and to interest him, but held back by the press of work and worry.

"It's Peters, really," Glenn told himself moving toward the door. "Solve Peters and you're in."

Doctor Crane had gone to great trouble to help a boy he didn't know. He'd taken in an outlaw horse when it was against everything he believed. So the doctor figured it was up to Glenn to pull hard—to bring this thing off. Maybe he thought Glenn could do it too, ease things along instead of getting mad, win over Peters when he couldn't. It made Glenn feel good. He'd made a dent in Crane after all.

But to solve Peters! Glenn moved toward the barn, shaking his head. That was tough. And Doctor Crane wasn't going to help. He was going to pour it on plenty, right along, Glenn could tell.

Glenn moved into the barn, sensing the struggle ahead with Peters, yet determined to see it through. He had to hold this job and go on to Ames. But right now, he had to get out to Peters and then back to Sky.

Tonight he was going to try to make Sky eat, for if

he did not, then it really looked bad for the roan. He was so thin it made Glenn shiver to see him.

In half an hour, with his own saddle and the saddle bags strapped behind the cantle, Glenn rode out of the yard, a hollow feeling at the pit of his stomach.

Barbara waved from the kitchen window.

Glenn waved back, then rode down Main Street and swung east, out of town along the St. Mary's.

At the edge of town, and up on the flat, stretching eastward to the roll of green hills, three boys on Indian ponies, with the big *B* brand on their hips, came out of the river bottom. Alongside Glenn's buckskin they rode, with Glenn not slackening his pace.

"Hello, Glenn," said Law-and-Order Clements, "you're goin' out to Peters'." His shrewd eyes studied Glenn's saddle bags. "To vaccinate calves," he added.

The other two boys nodded vigorously.

Glenn, with the grizzled rancher ahead to deal with, mustered a grin and tried to pass it off.

"Maybe," he said. "But anyway, Ricky, I'm in a hurry."

Ricky prodded his horse close to Glenn's.

"Watch your step," he warned. Then, with a glance at the other two boys, he added, "We'd better go with you."

Glenn couldn't shake an added moment of doubt even with Ricky's warning. He thrust it off.

"Now listen, Law-and-Order," he said. "You keep the peace around Cardston and leave Peters to me."

"Wait a minute. This vaccination is just a stall," Ricky warned. "Peters is really getting you out there to take you over the same as he did Larry Parks. Larry rode to vaccinate calves, too."

Glenn pulled his buckskin up short. In spite of himself Law-and-Order's words filled him with concern.

Well—he finally straightened in his saddle, trying to thrust his trouble off—let Peters try to take him!

"Peters had a right to offer Larry Parks good money, Ricky," he protested, with more assurance than he felt. "So long, and keep your scalp. There's plenty of Blood Indian kids who'd like to have that red pelt of yours for their belts."

Leaving the boys behind, but still pondering Law-and-Order's warning words, Glenn put spurs to Buck and rode swiftly toward the rolling hills ahead. Beyond them, and down the east slope lay Peters' range.

Along the roily banks of the Milk River, whose muddy water had given the river its name, lay the Peters' ranch: a set of log buildings with a house, a bunkhouse, a barn, and a series of pole corrals beyond them.

Down from the buildings lay the river, with deep swales leading to it. Swales deep and wide enough to hide half a hundred cattle from discovery. In these swales Peters thwarted the mange inspectors. A few head of cattle drifted up them, were missed by the riders, and spread the mange another year.

Reaching the top of the hill, Glenn paused a moment to sit his horse, looking down toward the Peters' ranch.

A slight dust hung over the corrals where four *Rolling R* punchers hazed a bunch of white-faced cows and calves into them. The dust, rising in a spiral, cast a slight haze over the sun. Glenn felt an uneasiness, and some of his confidence slipped from him.

The wild cries of the punchers increased this.

Rolling R punchers had a name for being wild. Peters' range was large and some funny things had been rumored about strangers riding across it.

Glenn squared his shoulders and, shaking Buck up with his reins, rode down the long slope toward the ranch.

Peters rode out to meet him. And there was something likable about the grizzled old rancher. He had level gray eyes under straight brows, and he knew his way around.

Right away he attacked, but in such a subtle way that Glenn hardly knew what to do.

Glenn reddened at his cordial greeting, thinking, Hey, this guy is smooth. He's no dumb bunny, smooth and deep.

Before he could adjust himself at all, Peters slid him farther down a trail that was as easy to descend as a dipping chute.

"How are you, Glenn?" he asked, extending a rope-gnarled hand and riding close to Glenn with his huge bay, sitting deep in his new saddle that was loaded with silver. He seemed to know all about Glenn's losses on the *Shoestring*, about Roy H, too, and how he had had to get out and look for work. He even knew about his wanting to go to Ames.

Glenn tried to get in a word; tried to let Peters know he was wise. For underneath his friendliness, Glenn felt a silken strength and grim purpose.

But Peters swerved his bay. A rolling tumbleweed fouled the bay's hind legs, all but dropping Peters as his horse threw a fit. Peters straightened in the saddle and, ignoring the whole thing, led Glenn down to the corrals.

Vaccinating was a thing of ease, too.

He'd expected a grudging bunch of punchers.

They were friendly, handling the chutes and the squeeze with deft ease and a speed that left Glenn pretty flat. Calf after calf went through the chute vaccinated.

In a lull, Peters motioned a rider over to the squeeze chute.

Glenn knew right away, looking at the slender blond boy, that he had signaled Larry Parks.

Peters said, "You know Glenn Barnes, Larry. He's taking your job with Doctor 'Crane."

In the pause that followed, Glenn couldn't help but look at Larry's pinto, also loaded with a silver-mounted saddle and a raw-silver inlaid martingale, and get the idea.

Peters might as well have said, "This is what you could have if you stayed here. This and double the ninety a month Doctor Crane is paying you."

It made Glenn wonder if he was crazy to keep on with Doctor Crane, even though he knew that he wasn't. He bent to his work, quiet, watchful, filled with a new and disquieting respect for this enemy. Filling his syringe with the required dosage of antitoxin, he walked over to the chute where a fat white-faced calf was held between two flat plank walls. Picking up a loose fold of skin just back of the shoulder, he plunged the needle deep, then with his thumb, injected the life-protecting serum.

Another calf followed, another, and still another, and Peters was always there helping, suave, quiet, suggesting by the way he treated his men that this was a good place to work.

Glenn, his mind awhirl, worked on in silence.

He'd expected to be treated to a frosty, "Hello!" He'd expected, too, to be able to open up on the subject of mange.

But Peters' manner headed him off. You'd have thought Peters would hand-ride every hill for every cow and dip her in the tile bathtub Glenn was sure Peters' bedroom had, if necessary, to comply with Crane's orders.

The fact was, he wouldn't, and had defied Doctor Crane, and Doctor Crane's predecessor before him.

It left Glenn helpless and tied as tight as a rodeo calf.

He finished vaccinating in silence. Cleaning up his syringe, with the calves finding their frantic bawling mothers out beyond the corrals, Glenn made a last try. The sun, a red ball, lay just above the blue Rockies to the south and west. Old Chief, backed by drifting clouds, stood bold in the foreground.

"Oh, Mr. Peters," Glenn began, intending to suggest a ride through part of his herd and a look out for mange.

But Peters shut him off.

He did it warmly, with his hand on Glenn's arm, as the boy finished packing his hypodermic needles in his saddle bags.

"We've prepared a little barbecue for you, Glenn," he said. "Cooked a yearling steer in a pit. A mange-free steer, I might say." His eyes sparkled, taking Glenn into his joke.

Glenn couldn't refuse.

He followed Peters down to his house and out onto

a terrace where Ling, the Chinese cook, stood smiling and bowing and calling him, "Doctee Barney."

The men, chaffing and easy, drifted in to sit at a long table. Peters sat at the head, motioning Glenn to a seat of honor at his right.

"Now, bring on that steer." Peters smiled.

Such food Glenn had never seen. Barbecued beef, canned California tomatoes, and fresh fruit from the Imperial Valley, ice cream from a home freezer, followed by fresh-frozen boysenberry pie and coffee, found their way almost by stealth to Glenn's plate.

"You see the way we eat at the *Rolling R?*" Peters' eyes asked Glenn

Glenn couldn't help eating.

"Boy, that's good," he said, sitting back from the table.

Then suddenly, a flicker of an eyelid did it. Peters' glance at Larry Parks tipped him off.

A sick feeling ran through Glenn. He realized that he'd been trapped. This was all a put-up job to lure him away from Doctor Crane.

Careful of his manners, but wondering how he could have been so dumb, Glenn rose. The remembrance of Sky, standing quietly in his stall, unable to eat, spurred him on.

"It's a long way to Cardston," he said, trying to move slowly. "Guess I'd better ride."

Still Peters had one more for him.

"You were going to say something to me out there by the corral?" the grizzled rancher asked.

Again Glenn felt a flush sweep up his neck to cover his face. He'd been going to suggest a look-see for mange, but now it was getting dark. Peters had seen that the meal lasted that long.

"Oh, nothing," Glenn was forced to say, then turned blindly toward the yard and Buck. He had been given the "business" and had fallen for it.

Mounting Buck, who'd been fed to the stuffing point, he said, "Thanks, Mr. Peters," and feeling the rancher's eyes on him, moved up toward the slope and toward Cardston.

Riding into the yard late that night, then on up to the barn, he shoved the door open and switched on the light.

His breath caught, and something like a low cry of contrition came from his lips. For Sky's hay lay untouched. The roan had not eaten, and he lay limply in his sling.

Moving into the stall, Glenn whispered, "Sky, you must eat." But his eyes roved around the shadowy barn and found no way to make him.

He moved up to the house to give a quick account of his trip to Doctor Crane. He put the instruments into the case, cleaned up, then came back to the barn.

The doctor hadn't pressed him about the mange.

Glenn was thankful, and knew that his struggle with Peters was going to be sharp.

8. Vat Inspection

AROUND the silent roan, Glenn moved, his heart heavy, his ears listening to the faint breathing of the weakening horse. Through the open barn door and across the darkness from Alan's room came the soft swing of music from Alan's accordion. Suddenly the roan's left ear twitched, and slowly he turned his head toward the sound.

Glenn knew there were horses who really liked music, Roy Rogers' horse Trigger loved it. But this was the first time Sky had taken an interest in anything since they'd put him in the sling.

A feeling of hope rose within Glenn. Then Sky turned his head back toward the full manger of fragrant hay and seemed to lose interest in the music. He couldn't last much longer, that was sure. Unless he picked up and started to eat soon Sky would starve.

Glenn stood there in the stall, not wanting to give up, yet baffled, not knowing what to do. The roan's foot, dressed by Doctor Crane, seemed no better either.

At length, Glenn slid an arm along the roan's neck, whispering, "Don't worry, Sky, I'll find a way." Then he moved toward the door.

Outside in the quiet dark, he paused a moment. A

soft wind blew down from the Rockies, drifting a-
round the corner of the barn with a low moaning
sound.

Glenn's heart felt squeezed shut. To lose Roy H,
and now Sky, was too much. He squared his shoulders. It wasn't going to be, that was all. He'd find a
way to make Sky eat.

Moving past the corral he picked his way toward
the lighted back porch. Barbara was away at her
young people's meeting at the United Church.

He moved on to his room and, throwing off his
clothes, opened the west window and slid quietly
under the covers. For a long time he lay, going over
the things he might do to Sky to swing the tide his
way. If he would only take an interest in life and act
as though he wanted to get well!

From the direction of the hospital the sound of
Alan's accordion persisted. Low and soft, it breathed
the slow melody of a strange song of plantation days.

Glenn slipped from bed to lean on the window sill.
It was sweet music; anyone would like it. At any other
time, he would have liked it himself. But the cold air
coming in the window made him shiver. Turning, he
slipped back into bed, rolling over on his side and
closing his eyes.

Late in the night he wakened from his sleep,
murmuring, "Maybe Sky would like Alan's music?"
A half-formed will to get up and rouse Alan flitted
through his mind. But he drifted off to sleep again.
"Tomorrow," he promised himself.

But in the morning, the hospital routine reached
out for Glenn. There were dogs to be fed.

Today the terrier's owner would come for him, and

that would be a relief. His yipping was beginning to get Glenn down.

Then there was the red setter's leg to cleanse, and the hound, operated on but yesterday, would need special care. Doctor Crane had gone in his Dodge to Daisy De Winton's *Confusion* ranch, grumbling, "That Daisy De Winton."

"She's bought a new prize bull she wants the doctor to pass on before she pays the money," Alan explained, with one of his rare smiles. "And she knows more about cattle than any woman in Alberta! I'm betting she'll grab that guy yet."

Glenn smiled with Alan and opened his mouth to suggest his playing for Sky. But Alan had gone on to the drying pen to see how the dogs were doing.

So Glenn went on with his feeding, wondering how he would ever get through until night, and realizing that Alan would probably turn him down anyway.

His morning work done at the hospital, Glenn had orders to ride out to the old dipping vat on the Blood Indian Reservation. He would look it over and send in a report to Stanley at the Standoff Agency about the repairs needed for the next dipping.

"Those people at Ottawa work pretty slowly," Doctor Crane had said. "We tell them now, and we're set for dipping. I intended going myself but I got this call. Drat that De Winton woman."

Glenn moved along the row of cages to one containing a black Angora cat, named Omar. A fishhook had caught in Omar's eye which had become infected.

"Hey, guy." Glenn poked his hand through the cage. "Don't get tough with me."

The black cat rolled over on its back pretending to bite him, scratching at his arm in mock fury.

At length, Glenn walked to the barn to saddle Buck for his ride. The filly in the first stall nickered softly as he came through the door.

Sky, in the third stall, did not move or turn his head.

Glenn could tell when a horse was about done as well as anyone. Now he moved in close, whispering, "See you tonight, Sky. Better get ready for that hot mash." Then because he was on Doctor Crane's time, he moved on to saddle Buck.

Barbara stood in the doorway as he came out. In her hand she held two brown-paper parcels and a small can of tomatoes.

"The cowboy's friend," she said, handing him the tomatoes, then the sandwiches. "I see by your face that Sky's no better," she added gently.

Glenn could not speak. His heart lay heavy within him.

"Did you have a nice time last night?" he asked, to avoid the subject.

"Yes." Barbara nodded. "Nice enough. But we need more new members like you and—" she stopped, her eyes troubled—"Alan," she added, "he's so fine. I want to get him to come to our meetings. He would be wonderful playing his accordion for us. He knows songs handed down from his grandfather who was a slave."

Glenn said, "For anybody, he's good."

Barbara nodded. "You know he has such new ideas about his people. He doesn't keep saying, 'The whites brought us here as slaves, let them work it out.'" She laughed. "He feels the responsibility for his own people. He says, 'The educated Negroes have as much responsibility for the Negroes' actions as the white people have.'"

Glenn nodded absently. The idea of getting Alan to play for Sky really took hold of him. He'd try it out tonight, ask Alan if he would do it.

To Barbara he said, "I'll see what I can do about getting Alan to go to your meeting." To himself he added doubtfully, "And playing for Sky."

Leading Buck outside, he swung into the saddle. "Well, so long," he said. "See you when I get back."

"Which will be about dark," Barbara answered, tossing her head.

"Can I help it if the vat's eight miles away?" Glenn asked, pushing Buck awake and toward the street. He rode west at a sharp running walk—the gait of any plainsman—wishing Sky were under him. The wind from Crow's Nest Pass to the west blew Buck's mane and pasted Glenn's windbreaker to his body. "Sky would like this," Glenn thought, watching white fluffy clouds scud before the wind.

A dun-colored coyote came from behind a ridge downwind and, getting no gun scent from Glenn, fell in behind.

Glenn rode for an hour due west, then cut north to the Bull Horn coulee. Riding this for half an hour he came to a swale through which the waters of a spring cut the Bull Horn.

There, beside a spring, he got off Buck and, dropping the reins to tie the horse western style, walked toward the dipping vat.

Reaching the vat Glenn studied the eighty-foot

length of it. Here in this vat, seven feet deep and two wide, and in an identical one east of Cardston near Peters' ranch, would be dipped all the cattle of this southern area, come fall.

Glenn picked up a pole and poked down into the brownish liquid residue of last year's dipping. A mixture of sulphur and lime, boiled five hours to form a medicinal bath deadly to mange, it now looked thick and it needed to be pumped out.

Here, last year, they had dipped under Doctor Crane's watchful eyes, and all the cattle of the Indian reserve had been put through with none missed.

But in the vat to the east, under the supervision of Larry Parks, cattle bearing the *Rolling R* of Peters had been missed.

Intentionally, some said. Glenn didn't know. But he determined, as he straightened up, that this fall's dipping would be different.

Glenn tossed the pole down, then took a survey of the vat sides which seemed in good repair. He walked through the system of corrals, noting a pole missing here and there, knocked off its pegs by some rampant steer whose hide tingled from the sulphur bath.

Glenn took a notebook from his pocket and sketched the necessary repairs needed, down to the last nail. The Blood Indians had to know in detail.

This done, Glenn slipped the bridle from Buck's head and let him graze.

Stretching himself out, sheltered from the wind by the vat side, he ate his lunch and the can of tomatoes. Finishing, he lay back, his head shaded from the sun's glare by his Stetson.

And there, suddenly, was the image of the weakened Sky before him. Glenn knew then that, come what may, he must get Alan to play. Yes, that very night.

"It's a last hope," he whispered, contrite that he hadn't asked Alan last night. The time lost might be serious.

Lying still was impossible now that he had made up his mind. Glenn leaped to his feet and, bridling Buck, mounted and rode east toward the long line of blue hills that formed part of Milk River Ridge.

Riding steadily, the coyote still trailing him, Glenn rode north of Cardston till at length he picked up the trail of yesterday. Three miles from the top of the rise down which he had ridden to Peters' ranch, he swung Buck north.

"No use picking up Peters today," he said. "We'll just look the vat over and send him the instructions about repairs. 'No use throwing acid in the eyes of a bull.'"

Glenn smiled wryly and pushed his horse ahead.

Riding north by east to the top of a ridge, then down a long slope, he reached the second spring. Beside it lay the second vat. Here, Glenn sensed, he would come to grips with Peters. Doctor Crane, by order of the Government, must supervise the Indian vat. That would leave this one for Glenn.

"Well." He shrugged, and moved down to the vat to inspect it in detail.

This vat, whether by chance or design of Peters, had been cunningly made to seem repaired, but was really in wretched shape. Posts rotted off below ground had not been replaced. Boards split and not renewed were dangerous to cattle confined in the corrals or swimming through the vat.

It took Glenn until sundown to finish his report. Stuffing the finished sheets in his saddle bag, he mounted and rode for town and Sky.

At dark he rode into the yard. Barbara, from her kitchen sink, the light shining on her blonde hair, called through the opened window, "Supper, Glenn, as soon as you can come. I've a meeting."

"Right away," Glenn promised, pushing on. He had to go to the barn to see if Sky had eaten.

But when he threw the door back and snapped on the light, he saw that the roan had not touched either hay or oats. Tending Buck, he felt as if a cold hand gripped his midriff.

"I've got to hurry," he breathed. "Got to get Alan."

Walking to the house, Glenn couldn't believe that he'd been here at the hospital nearly three weeks, and still the roan wasn't any better. He had thought that by now with Doctor Crane to help, the roan would be right on the trail.

Everything seemed unreal as he moved inside to wash and sit down at the table. The fried potatoes tasted like chips and all Glenn could think about was going out to see Alan.

"Dad's gone to Standoff to see a sick horse," Barbara said, sitting down at the table opposite Glenn. "Sometimes I think he'd be better off marrying Daisy." She sighed.

Glenn raised his eyes and with an effort concentrated on her words.

"Not till I get through Ames," he said. It was really a thought.

"Oh, so that's it," Barbara accused. "Running us right out of a job?"

Glenn reddened, his eyes protesting as he looked at Barbara.

"Don't answer that, Doctor Barnes," Barbara said, with a friendly smile. "It's just that I'm worried about his working so hard and Alan's refusing to go to the young folks' meeting next Sunday night."

Glenn stared at Barbara, a tightness in his throat. Sunday night was so soon, and by then Sky would be either on the road to recovery or—

"I'll see what I can do with Alan," Glenn promised Barbara. Rising hastily, he opened the door and walked through the lot to the rear of the hospital and paused at Alan's door.

At his knock, a voice said, "Come in."

Glenn opened the door and walked into Alan's room.

Alan, in gray slacks and a maroon shirt, sat on the edge of his cot bed. A braided rug, like the one in Glenn's room, lay on the floor. The whole room was furnished as well as Glenn's own. Above Alan's head on a shelf stood a picture of a pleasant woman in her early forties. Beside her stood a man of perhaps fifty-five, with a high forehead and good eyes.

Through the doorway Glenn could see a small kitchen.

On the table beside Alan stood a stack of books. Veterinarian books, Glenn saw. A book by Kriehbel shared prominence with Sinclair Lewis' *Kingsblood Royal*. The Bible, worn by much use, lay near at hand.

Alan rose as Glenn came in, and his questioning

eyes followed Glenn's which had moved back to the picture of the man and woman.

"My mother and father," Alan said quietly. But his manner said, "Of course you're not really interested, just curious."

For the same reason, and seeming to want to get rid of Glenn, Alan turned to a picture of a slight girl in an easel frame standing close to his pillow.

"Doris," he said. "She's working in a drug store in New Orleans until I get set."

Glenn could see that Alan thought it would be a long time, and that he didn't want to lose this job and make it longer. His feeling and understanding of Alan's jealousy made him sympathize with the colored boy.

But there was the matter of Sky and the accordion in its case by the table.

Seeking an opening for his subject, Glenn's eyes strayed to another picture. It was a faded crayon-drawing of an old woman sitting in a rocker before a stone fireplace.

"My great-grandmother," Alan said, his voice taking on a note of respect. "She was a slave on a New Orleans plantation. Her parents were brought from Africa and sold into slavery."

He paused once more as though to say, "Okay, Glenn, what's on your mind? Let's have it and then you can go."

Glenn could see that Alan had had a tough life. He had become hardened to loneliness, but never hardened to the condescending, comic-Negro attitude so often used against him.

Glenn knew then that he would get nowhere by

beating about the bush with Alan. He pulled a chair to him and sat down facing the quiet serious Negro boy.

"It's about Sky," he said.

"That outlaw?" Alan bristled. "I've done all I can for him. So has Doctor Crane."

"Have you?" Glenn leaned forward. "I guess you would change your mind if you could have seen Sky twitch his ears with pleasure that night you played."

Alan rose and, without a word, walked out to the kitchen for a drink, then back into the room. Glenn saw that his hands were trembling and his face set.

"It's crazy," Alan burst out at length. "That outlaw doesn't like music. He'd only like a hunk out of my right arm."

"It isn't crazy," Glenn pleaded. "Roy Rogers' Trigger likes music."

"Sure, but he's smart and civilized. He knows over a hundred tricks."

Glenn got up to face Alan. The slender Negro was a full four inches shorter than Glenn.

"No more civilized than Sky will be, or with more tricks up his sleeve," he said softly. "When I—I mean when we—get through with him." Putting a hand on the boy's arm, Glenn pleaded, "Come on, Alan."

Alan's face showed that he couldn't see going out to the barn with his accordion and playing for an outlaw horse.

"It's crazy," he repeated. "It will get around town that the clown Negro's ready for a comic circus role. Not on your life, I won't go, and that's final."

Glenn, watching Alan's face, knew that it was useless to argue. It had seemed so easy. He had thought it wouldn't be much for Alan to do, just go into a barn and play the *Blue Danube Waltz* or an old Southern song or two for Sky.

"Okay, Alan," he said dully and turned to leave.

9. Failure

GLENN walked across the lot to the barn, oblivious to the soft night wind, the myriad of twinkling stars overhead, and the wail of a coyote off toward the foothills west of Cardston. He reached the barn door, flung it open, and his heart filled with a kind of dull ache. He wondered, standing there with the wind fingering his hot face, if he would ever ride Sky on such a night. Would he sleep out under these stars, snug in his bag, with the blue roan picketed close by, and look up at the moon playing tag with floating silvery clouds across the night sky?

Glenn caught his breath, squared his shoulders and moved on into the barn. Sky had to get well, that was all there was to it. Alan had to come out and help.

But as Glenn walked into Sky's stall, the sick roan did not open his eyes. He lay in his sling, too weak to move, his breath barely moving the skin along his ganted flanks. And there was no sign of Alan.

Panic gripped Glenn, like a drawn lariat noose around a calf's throat. He fought it off and stooped to lift the roan's injured foot, unwinding the bandage with trembling fingers. The leg felt hot clear up above the knee, and the swelling, as the bandage came off, seemed as great as ever.

Glenn walked back to the hospital and brought a bucket of hot Lysol water. Putting the bucket close under the foot, he lifted it into the hot soothing water.

Sky did not protest, and barely moved when Glenn put his hand along the roan's ribs.

"If you only wanted to live," he whispered in the shadowy silence. "That's what is really wrong. You don't care."

Sky made no move.

Mechanically, Glenn went on bathing the roan's hot foot.

"Hey, Sky," he whispered, hardly knowing what he said. "You've got to get well. We've got things to do this fall. There are trips to the country. There's the dipping to oversee and Peters to win over."

But his words did not cause the roan to even twitch an ear. He just stood silent, head sagged, scarcely breathing.

At length Glenn pulled the foot from the hot water and dressed it as Doctor Crane had taught him. He went to get fresh hay for the manger, and then cleaned the stall of bedding, putting in fresh bright wheat straw underfoot. He ran fresh cold water in the bowl beside Sky's hot muzzle to tempt him. He got a bucket and, filling it with crushed oats, put it in Sky's feed box.

"Now, boy," he said, stepping back, his heart swelling with hope. "Eat, won't you? Eat your oats."

Sky did not even sniff at them.

Glenn leaned against the side of the stall looking at the roan, his ears alert for Alan's footsteps. Something had to be done, and soon. But standing there in the silence of the shadowy barn Glenn's panic deepened. Everything was so still.

The wind moaning around the corner of the barn sounded lonely. It was late. It must be almost eleven, and Sky's life was slipping away.

Glenn stood at Sky's head, too stunned to move.

He couldn't believe that something wouldn't save the roan. From the first moment down there in the river bottom until right now, he'd had but one idea: that he and Sky would ride the prairie together. They would work for Doctor Crane, meet Peters and bring him around to understand this mange fight. Sky would go back to the *Shoestring* and he would go on to Ames. Then they would meet here at Doctor Crane's again. Only then, it would be Doctor Glenn Barnes and Doctor Crane would be with Daisy De Winton.

Glenn put out a hand to Sky's sagging head, unable to believe that he couldn't save the roan, yet knowing that it must be so. For a horse, just as a human, had to want to live.

Hopelessly, trying one last thing, Glenn fished inside his windbreaker and brought out his harmonica. Heaving his body up into the manger in the sweet-smelling timothy hay, he lay back and put the mouth organ to his lips.

"I'll play the *Blue Danube*, Sky," he breathed, and putting the harmonica to his lips, he picked out the air of the lilting waltz.

But it wasn't much of a tune the way Glenn played it. It was thin and wiry and got lost in the silence of the barn, and Sky paid no attention.

All hope left Glenn then. He sat watching the roan sink lower and lower into the sling.

At last Glenn stowed his harmonica in his wind-breaker again and climbed out of the manger. Back beside the roan, he touched the limp foretop of the outlaw, his eyes wet, his heart throbbing, and his mind telling him that the horse was a goner, and that Alan was certainly not coming.

He put his arms around Sky's neck and pulled him close.

"Don't quit the range yet, Sky," he pleaded. "Stick around till round-up time, boy."

He stood there, losing track of time, holding the horse to him.

Suddenly from the direction of the doorway came the sound of soft music, the plaintive notes of the old slave song that Alan had played the first night Glenn had heard him.

Glenn couldn't believe his ears. He swung to face the colored boy, hope filling him anew for Sky's chances.

"Alan," he breathed. "You came after all."

Alan came toward him, his fingers slipping over the keys of the black accordion strapped to his slim frame, but his eyes held doubt and a resentment.

"Yes, I came." He nodded, and went on playing the slave song, then swung to *My Old Kentucky Home* and *Dixie*.

Sky did not move or let on that he had heard.

Alan moved closer, his nimble fingers weaving the sad melody of the New Orleans levee: *Roll that Bale*.

Still Sky's head sagged. His muzzle made no move

toward the cold water, or the sweet-smelling, life-giving hay in the manger.

Glenn caught the manger for support. Was it possible that even Alan's music couldn't bring Sky back? He felt his throat go dry.

He swallowed, then managed to say hoarsely, "Try him on the *Blue Danube*, Alan."

Alan shifted the accordion and, nodding, struck a note of the waltz. He played a dozen bars.

Sky did not move a muscle. His breath seemed to have stopped entirely.

Glenn held his own breath, then called, "More, Alan, and louder."

Alan pulled the accordion to him and, pumping vigorously, shot into the swift swirling motion of the *Blue Danube*.

For a full minute it seemed as though time hung suspended. It was, Glenn thought, like when the bucking chute swings open, before the bucking horse realizes he is free.

A bat flew out of the darkness of the rafters, swinging low over them. The filly in the next stall nickered.

Glenn's eyes could only watch the roan.

No, the horse was through.

Glenn turned to the plank side of the stall. How long he stood there he did not know.

A new sound brought him to. Sky was drinking!

Turning his head, Glenn brushed his eyes in disbelief. He had given up hope, but now Sky was drinking.

Glenn still couldn't believe it when Sky's muzzle found some hay wisps and ate them, then went on to take a second drink, at first exploratory, then buried deep in the cool dark water of the bowl.

A thought spilled over into Glenn's mind like mountain water over high rocks. Sky would live to take Roy H's place! They would ride the plains together. Sky would grow fat and sleek: a real sky-blue roan with the sun glistening on his sides.

"Sky, Sky," he whispered. "You are going to live!"

Even as he spoke a step sounded in the quiet, from the opened barn door. Glenn turned to face the sound, catching a fleeting glimpse of a dark heavyset man with a scar across his left cheek.

Before he could look again, the man had gone.

Glenn's mind told him: "He heard me say Sky's going to get well. Does that man own my sky-blue horse? Does he?"

Glenn sprang to the door to stop him. They could make a dicker if he did. There was nothing to greet Glenn's troubled eyes but the shadowy form of a man mounting a horse and riding off into the night.

Slowly Glenn came back to the barn and Sky. He watched Sky's cropped ears lying back along his head. Did Sky know and hate this stranger?

Glenn wished he had caught a closer look at the man's face, so that he might recognize him again. He wished, too, the stranger had come in and talked it over.

Was the man going to wait till Sky sleeked up, then come for him? Perhaps throw him back on the rodeo circuit once more? Make a killer of him again?

Doggedly Glenn gathered more hay for Sky's manger. He move to bed down his stall. There was just one thing to do—keep fighting. Get on with his job here, working hard for Doctor Crane and trying to win Alan's friendship.

With a last pat on Sky's neck, Glenn turned toward the door and, with Alan following, moved out of the barn.

At the corral gate, Glenn turned to Alan.

"Thanks," he said. "You were swell to help. Maybe we can teach Sky tricks when he gets well."

Alan shifted the weight of his accordion. It seemed that he wanted to be friendly, yet wondered if he weren't being used, as usual.

"It's okay," he said. "I did it because Doris would have wanted me to."

"Sure." Glenn put out a hand.

Again Alan tightened up. "But at that," he said, "it's kind of silly getting a horse well and teaching him tricks for another man to come and claim."

10. Sky Takes Over

BEFORE daybreak some mornings later, Glenn lay tossing on his bed. A recurrent drumming noise, like the beat of cattle hoofs in hard ground, kept running through his head.

He turned on his belly, burying his head in the pillow.

The pounding continued.

"Go 'way," he murmured, and turned over.

The sound became clearer as the eerie half-dawn light came in his window.

Glenn sat up, and suddenly knew what it was!

"Sky," he exclaimed, leaping from his bed. "It's Sky banging in his stall!"

Hoping his hunch was wrong, he threw on his clothes and went out to the barn and Sky.

Stepping over the sill, he knew with sinking heart that his hunch had been correct: Sky was on the mend, but he was also on the warpath.

Glenn walked toward the stall with the sound of Sky's foot cracking the stall beside him.

There, hung on a nail as it must have been ripped from a coat, was a red and blue piece of mackinaw cloth.

Ricky Clements happened by, and, seeing the careful way Glenn handled the colored scrap, sensed a mystery.

"It's a clue," Law-and-Order said, coming inside, his brown eyes staring at the cloth. "It's something for our club to work on."

Glenn lifted the cloth from the nail, surveying it. It was a clue all right. A clue not only to the stranger, who must have come back to look at Sky, but to the roan's behavior.

Drawing the boy aside, he gave him the story, as much of it as he knew. Law-and-Order promised to do his best. Yes, he'd noticed the man around.

Glenn's worry deepened.

For weeks the horse had been sick and mean. Now with this stranger showing up, he'd suddenly become worse than ever. Something deep within him, born of fear and hatred, seemed to have boiled to the surface.

Sky tried to bite Glenn as he moved into the stall. He reared and snorted at the smell of the bit of torn coat in Glenn's pocket.

"That stranger must have been Sky's owner," Glenn decided. That meant he'd better get busy and tame this horse and earn money to buy him when the man came back. Balleau? How did you talk to a man like Balleau?

"Easy, Sky," Glenn soothed, moving close to him. He promised with more assurance than he really felt, "you have friends here. I'm not going to slug you with a quirt. I'm not going to let that man take you away."

Sky turned his head, some terrible memory strong

within him. His teeth swiped Glenn's arm with a vicious ripping sound.

Glenn flung his arm away, misery within him. He had to make this horse like him. They had work ahead with Peters.

"No, Sky," he said, examining his sleeve for a tear, "I'm your friend."

Sky had gone back to his colthood. The blood of the wild stallion that had sired him came surging to the surface. The memory of nights filled with skulking wolves and days spent fleeing the hated man-smell, high in the foothill country of the Rockies, formed a mist of hatred before his eyes.

As Glenn left the stall to get him oats, Sky lashed out at him with murderous black heels.

They caught Glenn fair, sending him catapulting across the barn floor and against the planks of an opposite stall. Fortunately, Sky was still in his sling and hadn't too much strength in his kick.

Glenn got up, brushing the straw from his clothes.

"Okay, Round One for you," he said, moving on to get the oats, then coming back in beside the horse. But putting the can of oats in the box and preparing to brush the roan's coat down, Glenn heard another footstep. It was Larry Parks of the *Rolling R.*

Glenn stuffed his hands into his pockets, feeling the bit of cloth which he must divide with Law-and-Order who might pick up something around Cardston, and waited for Larry to open up.

Larry said, "Peters is buying two hundred head of cattle from the Calgary yards, and he doesn't figure on dipping them." He paused, his blue eyes measuring Glenn.

Glenn carefully kept quiet. He wasn't going to give Larry a thing to take back to Peters.

"Of course you could slap a quarantine on his cattle," Larry suggested hopefully.

And make an enemy of Peters for life, Glenn thought. Oh, no. I want to wind up this thing with Peters a friend. I want to practice around here.

He moved carefully over to the wall and, taking up a currycomb and brush, moved back to Sky. He would wait Larry out, then proceed with Sky's training.

Larry leaned against the stall.

"He aims to ship them in here," he said, "then trail them out to the *Rolling R* and kick them loose. He's within his rights, too."

Glenn ran the currycomb through Sky's thick black mane. "Yeah, I know," he agreed.

" 'Cause cattle are given a clean bill of health at the yards in Calgary." Larry probed on.

"Sure," Glenn nodded. But if mange is to be swept from the range here, they'll have to be dipped again this fall, he added to himself.

"Maybe he'll trail them overland," Larry suggested. "He could bring them in by Macleod and across the reserve."

"Sure," Glenn agreed. And spread mange all the way through the Indian bunch, he added to himself. Peters would do it, too, unless some way were found to check him.

Larry moved closer to Glenn, then stepped back, paling slightly before the wind of Sky's flying hoofs.

"I—I was going to say," he faltered, "Peters thinks it's all silly, this thing of getting rid of mange. He thinks you're too smart to fall for it, and he wants you to work for him."

Glenn soothed Sky with a pat on his neck, then turned to Larry. He liked him. They had gone to the same school in Macleod. They had ridden in the Calgary Stampede together. And he could think of lots of worse things than working for Land Peters, except that he had a job. Brother, did he have a job! Taming this outlaw and convincing Peters in a friendly way that he'd better buckle under.

"Sorry, Larry," he said.

"The grub's good," Larry argued, but took the hint and began to walk toward the door.

"And good wages—hundred and eighty a month, which is twice what you're making here."

Glenn, hiding his impatience, grinned. "Twice it is."

But Larry could see that it was no go.

"What'll I tell Peters?" he blurted finally. And Glenn knew that it had been Peters' idea.

"Tell him," Glenn said, after a moment's thought, "that the next meal will be on me." He paused, then walked close to Larry, his eyes steadily fixed on the wavering ones of the *Rolling R* rider. "Tell him, too," he added, taking a deep breath, "that he's going to dip those Calgary cattle and like it."

"Yeah?" Larry's eyes widened.

"Yeah." Glenn gulped, feeling silly, yet sticking his ground.

Through the fading patter of Larry's horse going down the road, Law-and-Order's voice came hushed and wondering from the shadows where he had been standing.

"How you goin' to do that?" he demanded.

Glenn mustered a grin. "I—I don't know," he admitted. "But there must be some way."

"Sure." Law-and-Order's voice quavered in response. "Sure thing. And now that clue? You goin' to give me half of it? I've a few ideas, and the club guys will work on it."

Cutting the cloth in two, Glenn gave half of it to Ricky, then, stuffing the other half in his pocket, turned back to Sky.

"If you get anything, Law-and-Order," he called to the red-headed boy, "let me know, but quick."

"Sure," Ricky called back and was gone.

Glenn turned to Sky, grooming him with the comb and brush, slicking him up for the day. As he worked, his mind mulled over Larry's visit, then went on to figure ways to bring Peters around. Nothing seemed to come, no plan that would work.

No plan, either, seemed to make any impression on Sky, who remained as wild and untamed as ever.

Days passed—a week, two, then Glenn lost count.

The roan now was out in the corral, sleek and fat, his foot healed, but his disposition unchanged.

Glenn, in despair, watched from outside of the plank corral, leaning back when the roan rushed at him, his body hitting the planks in his effort to get at Glenn.

Jensen, the town blacksmith, came out of the evening shadows to stand by Glenn.

"He is one bad actor," he said, scratching his thinning blond hair with a grimy sooted hand. "Maybe he never be tamed, Glenn. Maybe he always be outlaw." He stared through the planks at the rushing roan.

Glenn knew that something would have to happen soon.

"You know that scar's a bad thing on his foot," Jensen said, shaking his head once more, and his voice died away. Suddenly it picked up. "You know, Glenn, I bane thinkin', maybe we fit shoes on that horse. Maybe that scar hurts him and makes him ornery?"

Glenn stood beside the corral, his hands on the planks that still quivered from Sky's last charge.

He debated Jensen's idea and he was desperate.

Jensen's voice went on.

"You know, Glenn, that horse is two horses. There is the deep down horse that rodeos have made. The killer horse who wants to fight back. Then there is the nice horse who wants to be friends. Maybe we put shoes on him and bring them together."

"With work?" Glenn asked hopefully.

"Maybe?" Jensen agreed.

The soft music of Alan's accordion came form his room.

"Or music?" Glenn added. It sounded fantastic.

"Could be." Jensen nodded. "Anyway, tomorrow, if you say so, we put shoes on him."

Glenn looked through the planks to study the sleek roan. The last rays of the setting sun were lighting his coat and finding the fighting gleam in his flashing eyes as Sky reared before him. He had to swing Sky into line.

"Shoes it is," he said.

So early the next night Glenn, with Jensen to help,

roped Sky and took him down to Jensen's shop. With the hoist they gently lifted the fighting roan's four feet off the ground. Jensen pared off the hoofs and fitted him with shoes. He made a special shoe for the tender foot, working carefully over the anvil with the red-hot iron, fashioning a shoe slightly curved to take care of the deformity.

"There," he said, when he had finished. "Now, you banc good horse. You behave."

Sky's answer, once the hoist let his four feet to the ground, was to kick a row of tools to the blacksmith's floor, bolt through the shop door and, with tail up, streak for his barn.

Jensen, standing with arms on his leather apron, stared after the horse, then turned doubtful eyes to Glenn's.

"You never tame him," he said. "He is outlaw till the end."

Glenn stubbornly refused to believe that this could be.

He walked up the street of Cardston with the wind blowing smartly from the west, until he came to the hospital. There must be some way to find the heart of this roan beauty.

But as he walked through the corral toward Sky's stall, Doctor Crane came into his office to stand in the doorway.

"Oh, Glenn," he said, and there was an urgency in his voice that Glenn had never noticed before. "Ride out to Daisy De Winton's with me, will you? One of her prize heifers broke off a horn. I'll have to treat it; may need your help."

"To escape Daisy," Barbara whispered, coming up. "Go on, Glenn."

Glenn sat beside the tall gaunt doctor, his mind shuttling between Sky and some way to tame him, and Doctor Crane and Daisy, as they rode out along Lee's Creek to Daisy's ranch house.

Getting out of the Dodge, he couldn't restrain a whistle.

"Some shebang!" he breathed, glancing toward the ranch house of low white siding, lying snugly under a hill. Then he looked across a bridge to the barns, blue and white and spotless in the gathering dusk.

"You think so?" Doctor Crane's eyes probed Glenn's as he took up his bag to go toward the house.

Glenn watched half a dozen white-faced cows, sleek and blooded, standing in a meadow. Opposite, in a corral, stood two priceless bulls, bellowing moodily into the gloom.

"Sure do," Glenn said, and suddenly wondered why Doctor Crane didn't give in to Daisy.

She came now from the house, dainty, with flying blonde hair, dressed in green jodhpurs and a yellow sweater. It was evident that she liked the doctor. Frankly she wanted him to like her, to come to live at *Lonely Willows* ranch.

"Hello, Doctor. Hello, Glenn," she said, her brown eyes big and round like the flower for which she was named.

"Hello, Daisy," Doctor Crane said shortly, taking her hand because he couldn't escape it. "Where's this cow? I've just eaten supper and I have ten things to do yet tonight."

"Heifer, not cow," Daisy said with a humoring smile

and a look at Glenn. "Fleurette, out of Flossy, by Hector."

Turning, she led the way down a path, across a bridge and to the big blue barn. Four attendants in smart white uniforms with *Lonely Willows* in blue across their backs came to the door as they walked up.

Glenn couldn't help but smile at the doctor's nickname for Daisy's ranch. There certainly wasn't any confusion here. The confusion was all in Doctor Crane's mind, Glenn decided.

"She's broken her horn and I wanted you to be sure there's no infection," Daisy explained, leading the way to a stall. "She caught it in the stanchion."

A sleek two-year-old heifer stood with her left horn dangling by some skin.

Doctor Crane moved in beside the whiteface carrying his bag.

"The stump'll have to be smoothed up," he said. "Daisy, you wait up at the house."

"I'll wait right here," she said.

Glenn couldn't help admiring her as they put the heifer's head in a locked stanchion. It would be bloody work and painful.

Daisy watched until Doctor Crane, with the suitable saw for the purpose, smoothed the stump, then applied disinfectant.

"It will bleed some," he said, "But not excessively. And it will purify the wound."

Determinedly, against the wishes of Daisy who wanted him to come up to the house to wash, he moved to a spigot across the runway of the barn.

There, in silence, he washed his hands, dried them

on a towel brought from his bag, and with a hurried, "Alan will sterilize the instruments," piled them all in the black bag and moved for the door.

Back at the car, with Daisy trailing, he put out his hand. "Good night, Daisy," he said, ignoring her pouting. "If anything develops—which it won't—call me up."

In five minutes, with Glenn sitting beside him, the doctor fled *Lonely Willows* ranch and drove along Lee's Creek toward home.

"Drat that woman." Doctor Crane turned the wheel to avoid a rock in the road. "I came out here from Ontario to do an important job."

Glenn did not speak; he was getting some insight into what the doctor was driving at. He was no quitter.

"I worked hard to put myself through Ames," the doctor went on. "I studied night and day in Friley Hall."

Glenn drew his breath in. Friley Hall, where he'd live. Perhaps he'd get Doctor Crane's room.

"I dreamed of helping save children's lives with tuberculin tests for cows and Bang's disease serum. I wanted to ease the pain of animals that can't talk and tell you where they hurt."

Glenn nodded. Deep within him, that was the way he felt. It was wonderful to know that the doctor did too.

"I wanted to raise the standards of veterinarian practice," Doctor Crane went on. "To make it mean something besides being a horse doctor." His foot pushed the throttle to the floorboard. "I wanted to make the world respect us."

"And lick Peters in an honest fight," Glenn whispered to himself.

"And I'm not ready to cave in to Daisy De Winton. Not yet, at any rate."

Glenn felt the car sway and they moved into their own yard. A tingling sensation crawled up his back as he got out of the car, and he felt a renewed strength for the fight ahead.

Crane was a great man. He wasn't taking the easy way out. He had been sent out here to do important work and he was sticking with it.

"Yes, Doctor," he managed huskily. "I know what you mean."

The older man and the boy stood in the quiet darkness. Nothing but the purr of the motor disturbed the quiet of the place.

It was a precious moment for Glenn that he was to remember all the years of his life. Doctor Crane had taken him into his confidence. He had told him he was sticking. He had implied that Glenn might too.

Glenn felt elated. He knew, too, that he must find some way to tame the roan; that a way would come to him. Then he would go on to help Doctor Crane with Peters.

Unwilling to break the silence, he stood there.

Suddenly a dog down the street barked.

The doctor moved abruptly to get his bag.

"Well, what are we standing here for?" he growled.

Glenn said, "I'll put the car away, Doctor."

Doctor Crane nodded curtly and moved toward his office.

Glenn drove the Dodge into the garage and, shutting off the motor, crawled from the car.

Closing the garage doors, he moved across the lot and through the corral to the barn. Snapping on the light, he stood a moment, looking at the roan, a question in his eyes.

In his stall Sky swung his head, laid back his ears, then turned back to his hay, and seemed to say, "Scram!"

Glenn went toward him, his elation oozing from him.

Sky laid back his ears, and again turned to eat a wisp of timothy. Glenn moved in beside him, and something hurt within him.

"You are two horses," he said, "as Jensen figured you. Two horses that are worlds apart."

He stood a moment, running the roan's silken mane through his fingers, pondering how to bring them together.

Suddenly on the night air came the sound of Alan's accordion. Sky turned his head, flicked his ears, and seemed to like it. But it was only the liking of an instant.

Glenn, recalling the night they had been together in the barn and Alan had played for him, whispered, "I wonder, Sky. Would music tame you down for the work?"

He swung to the door and stood there a moment surveying the surly roan before turning off the light.

"No, I guess not," he said. Then he snapped off the light, closed the door and went to his room. And there, propped against the lamp, lay a card from Abbie.

Glenn slumped to the bed. For a moment he

studied the spare neat handwriting of the foster mother who meant so much to him. He read:

Dear Glenn:

We are not going to move after all. I will write you soon and tell you all about it. We are both glad you got the job with Doctor Crane. Luce is well. We both send our love.

Abbie B.

Glenn sat staring at the card, considering. Should he send them some money now? They must need it. But then he put the card in a drawer beside his bed and began to undress. No, he'd wait for Abbie's letter. That would be time enough.

11. He Fools Glenn

THE NEXT morning Glenn wakened early and, slipping into his clothes, walked out to the kitchen for breakfast. The time had passed, he sensed, when he could spend much time with the roan. Doctor Crane had been tolerant with him while Sky was sick, but now, with the crisis past, he would have to stick to business. And of course the business was Land Peters and making him come around on dipping.

The uncertainty about Peters was running Doctor Crane ragged and it lay like a thorn just under Glenn's plaid shirt.

Glenn walked over to the washstand to douse his face in cold water and dry it. He ran a comb through his thick rust-red hair, and then sat down at the table.

Doctor Crane already sat opposite him, his lean hands holding the *Calgary Herald,* his eyes on the page.

"Good morning," Glenn said, hoping that the warmth between him and the doctor would carry over from the night before.

"Good morning," the doctor replied, scarcely looking up. It was the only time he had to himself, and then only a few minutes.

Glenn knew this and didn't mind.

110

Barbara came across the kitchen with a stack of hot cakes for the doctor and a bowl of oatmeal for Glenn.

"What do you think?" she asked. "Alan's dodging coming to meeting with me."

Doctor Crane's eyes stayed on his paper.

Glenn poured cream on his porridge and took up his spoon. Alan was all right, underneath. But he had his own ideas.

"Don't rush him, Barbara," Glenn advised, taking a spoonful of porridge. "He's got things on his mind. He's helping his father and trying to save enough to go to school and to get married. When you're that busy you don't have time to go to meetings."

Barbara tossed her head, then put three little round cakes on the skillet. Their zing came to Glenn.

"If he were a white boy he'd have come by now," Barbara said. With a sweep of her spatula, she flipped the cakes over.

Glenn nodded. "Maybe so, but I still think he's too busy. Give him time."

In silence he ate the three cakes Barbara brought him, then pushed back from the table and stood up.

"Oh, yes," Doctor Crane said, looking over the paper, "Alan has the flu. I forgot to tell you. You'll have the feeding and extra work this morning, Glenn."

Glenn nodded and slipped out the door. Going to the hospital, he took a quick look at Alan, lying quiet and feverish.

"Barbara's going to fix you up," he said. Then he went on into the hospital.

In a few minutes Doctor Crane's step sounded, going into his office.

Glenn, mulling over the roan's reactions to music, and the problem of Peters, moved swiftly through the morning's routine. It seemed less lonesome around the hospital now with another terrier to take the place of the yippy one who'd gone home.

This new one had a torn lip.

"Too close contact with a porcupine," Doctor Crane had said, sewing it up. But the lip hadn't kept him from barking.

The hound had gone back to Peters, too, and the silken-haired setter back to Harmon of the *Double Anchor.*

By the time Glenn had put the dogs out in their runs, scrubbed the kennels and the floor with Q.A. antiseptic, patients were coming in.

A man came through the door carrying a golden-brown Chesapeake retriever. It was King Benton of the hill country, who made his living with hunting dogs.

"I was backing my car out of the garage, Doc," he said. "Rory, here, was lying asleep."

He laid the dog on the operating table. The retriever was quiet except for spasms of shivering and an occasional jerk. He had a clouded look in his eyes.

Glenn had seen enough around the hospital to know that the big brown dog was suffering from shock.

"I'll want him under the fluoroscope," Doctor Crane said. "Lift him over here, Glenn."

He pulled the blinds down and snapped on the fluoroscope as Glenn lifted the retriever to a second table. Against the plate, the slim bones of the injured leg showed a clear fracture below the hock.

"Fortunately, the car didn't pass over his body," the doctor said, passing the stethoscope over the dog in a deft rapid examination. "Now to set the leg. We'll use a traction splint."

Glenn held the dog as Doctor Crane injected the anesthetic with deft hands.

"Four cc's of nembutal," he explained to Glenn who watched intently. Something of the importance of Doctor Crane to the people around here came again to Glenn. Benton made his living with dogs like Rory. They depended on Doctor Crane.

"I inject it into the radial vein," Doctor Crane went on. "The amount of anesthetic is governed by the size of the dog, and Rory here's a big dog."

Turning, he put the emptied hypodermic needle back on its pad along with two others.

"A heart stimulant and an antidote for the nembutal, in case we give too much," Doctor Crane explained in answer to Glenn's questioning eyes.

Applying his stethoscope, the doctor listened to Rory's heart. "Kicking right along," he said. "He'll be out in a short time."

Glenn watched Rory's eyes, seeming to notice that the pupils dilated, then contracted.

Doctor Crane opened the dog's mouth. It did not close.

"He's out," he said. "But to make sure, I'll try this." Taking up one of the retriever's forefeet, he pinched the skin between the toes. "No reaction. I can set the leg now.

"Fortunately, the fracture did not come through the skin," the doctor was instructing Glenn as he worked. "Now for the traction splint." Taking a wire rod, he bent it to form a frame for the leg, then proceeded to fasten the leg within it, keeping it straight, so the edges of the broken bone would just touch and knit together.

When he had finished, the doctor motioned Glenn to carry the dog back to the fluoroscope. Once more under the flickering light in the darkened room, the doctor checked the set.

"Seems fine," he said, putting on more binding and an outer wrapper over both frame and leg. "Put him in number four kennel, Glenn. Let him come out gradually."

"Will he be all right for the opening of the duck season?" Benton asked anxiously. "I have some Hollywood men coming for the fifteenth of September. I'll need Rory then."

Doctor Crane smiled slightly, then nodded. "I think so," he said. "We'll do the best we can."

King Benton turned to go, and Glenn, watching his face, saw how grateful he was to Doctor Crane.

Suddenly a new, a deeper meaning to the doctor's life came to Glenn.

"He's a missionary here," he whispered, gently carrying Rory back to his kennel. "He's wonderfully kind, really. And he's doing the only thing that counts in this world, helping people and animals out of trouble."

Putting Rory gently down in the iron net-work kennel, Glenn shut the door with strong hands.

When he turned around there was Larry Parks again, dressed in a red flannel shirt and white cords. Out behind him and through the door, Glenn could see his saddle horse and beside it a pack horse.

"I'm going fishing for three days, Glenn," he said. "How would you like to come along?"

Glenn's mouth dropped open. It was about the last thing in the world he wanted right then.

"Leave this?" he demanded. "For a fishing trip?"

Suddenly he knew how closely bound he was to this place. Why, it was like part of his body, a leg or an arm.

"Oh, no," he said. "Sorry, Larry." The thought of Sky came sharp and sure, and the importance of making something of the big blue horse. Beyond that lay Peters and the battle to bring him into line on dipping his cattle right.

Glenn stood watching Larry's tall slim blond figure go out of the yard and mount his horse.

"I've got to make time," he said. "Doctor Crane isn't going to put up with Sky's tantrums forever. Sooner or later, he'll say, 'Make good with this outlaw or get out, both of you.'"

But it was some time before Glenn could find time to go back to Sky.

Then one evening, after dinner, with the wind blowing softly from the west, and ducks winging in the evening twilight to their nesting places, he walked across the lot and to the corral gate.

"This is it, Sky," he said, watching the blue horse turn to face him. "This is where you start to live right."

Sky's answer was to move swiftly across the corral, his black hoofs churning the powdered ground, his sleek body catapulting twelve-hundred pounds of muscle against the planks.

He turned and reared a straight column of beauty

in the evening air, and came down on all fours. He lashed out with his hind feet, splintering the top plank and sending its pieces flying past Glenn's head.

He stood, tail up, head erect, and whistled with a huge snort on the wind.

Glenn caught his breath, watching.

"What a horse!" he whispered. "What a horse to ride! What a horse to rope from, fast as chain lightning, and solid as a cliff in a pinch!"

Moving to the gate, Glenn opened it and stepped inside. Sky rushed him. He came with such force that Glenn knew it would be suicide to stick.

With a quick movement, he stepped outside and closed the latch.

The gate bulged with Sky's weight against it.

Glenn got his lariat and tried to rope the horse.

Sky ducked his head and circled the corral at high speed. His coat lathered, his eyes gleamed in the setting sun.

Then softly, from Alan's room, came the sound of music. It was the *Blue Danube Waltz* and it swelled out on the night air.

It came closer, and suddenly there was Alan standing beside the corral, the accordion strapped to him, his fingers playing over the keys.

The effect on Sky was magical.

He trotted to the fence, thrusting his muzzle through the planks. He moved back, flicking his cropped ears at the sound. He ran across the corral, then came back with express-train speed to plow into the dirt, sending it flying over Alan and Glenn.

Glenn, coiling his lariat, opened the gate and walked in beside Sky.

The big horse let the rope go over his ears to form a loop. He permitted a second loop to form an Indian hackamore. He let Glenn lead him around the corral to the sound of Alan's music.

Excitement burbling through his voice, Glenn said, "Keep playing, Alan," and ran for his saddle.

Sky let him come into the corral and slip the Navajo blanket on his sleek back. He let him put the saddle on and cinch it.

Then, with a swift glance at Glenn and another at Alan, he put his head down and really went into it.

"Look out!" Law-and-Order yelled from the top pole of the corral. He had come from his house across the street.

It was good advice.

Sky sunfished. He bawled and bellowed. He ran the circle of the corral at high speed. He kicked the top pole off the corral and, ducking his head, bucked some more.

He bawled till Jensen came, and the doctor from his room, and another man with a scar who looked through the bars a second, then faded into the night, muttering with satisfaction, "He's ready. I'll take him for the rodeo circuit now."

Glenn stood watching his saddle loose its moorings and go flying across the corral top.

A sort of sickness went through him.

Sky had been cured. He'd been given care and attention, and what was he?

"An outlaw," the doctor's trembling, outraged voice declared beside him, "an outlaw who will never be anything else."

12. Sky Loses Glenn's Job

GLENN waited until the doctor moved off into the long dusk of an Alberta summer evening. It seemed then, going to pick up his saddle, leading Sky back into the barn, bedding him down for the night and going on to his room, that his world caved in on him. The doctor, he knew, had just about had his fill, and no wonder.

Peters, coming through the opened barn door, put it right when he said, "Well, that was quite a ruckus Sky put up out there, wasn't it? The doctor liked it, didn't he?"

Glenn climbed into the mow to throw down more hay for Sky, not trusting himself to answer. When he came down to stand by Peters, he nodded.

"No, he didn't, but I don't blame him."

Peters came right to the point. "Oh, well, he'll soon be out of here anyway. I'm running in a bunch of cattle from Calgary and I'm not dipping them now or this fall."

Glenn paused. Hot words flowed to his lips. He choked them back.

"Take it easy," a voice within him warned. "You will need this man's friendship some day."

"No?" he managed softly.

"No," Peters said with equal quiet. "And when the

Government at Ottawa gets wind of it, Crane will be on his way."

Glenn faced Peters. They stood toe to toe, about the same height and weight; Glenn fair and full of grit, with a shock of red hair; Peters dark, his bullet head covered with a gray shock of hair; both set with purpose.

"Of course, if you think that's fair," Glenn said, "and you're sure that mange can't be swept from the range."

"It's fair because it can't be," Peters said shortly. "Let's quit quibbling around with these doctors with stars in their eyes and get a practical man. One who'll face the fact that mange is here to stay."

Glenn still held back his anger. He just walked to Sky, patted the roan's neck a moment, then moved toward the barn door.

Peters took Glenn's silence for a sort of consent.

"And that brings me to my proposition," he said, walking close to Glenn. "Come out to the ranch and work for me. I'll pay you two hundred a month. It'll send you to Ames. You can graduate and come back here to practice."

Glenn stood taking it all in. Peters was pretty smooth, thinking to get his own man back here to be veterinarian and not make any more trouble.

Peters thought Glenn had agreed.

"You can even bring Sky," he said.

Glenn put his hand cautiously on the barn door to close it. Peters was a power here. He had to be turned down easy, and not be made sore, for beyond this talk lay the battle. One which he must win in a way as smooth and subtle as Peters himself.

Sure he was going through Ames. Sure he was coming back here to practice—but with Peters whipped into line and mange on the run.

"Let me ask you something, Peters," Glenn said, trying to keep his voice quiet. "If you were in my place would you do this to Doctor Crane?"

In the silence that followed, Glenn watched the red crawl up Peters' neck, even darkening his wind-burned face a deeper shade.

He'd said the wrong thing, he knew then.

"All right. Glenn," Peters' voice came like the cut of a loaded quirt. "You asked for it. The fight is on. My next move will be two hundred trailing cattle shoved on the range undipped."

Glenn should have let him go. He knew that later as he lay in bed, thinking it out. But now, he raced after the cowman's departing footsteps, and stood beside him as he mounted his big bay horse.

"Oh. no, it won't, Peters," he heard his voice say. "You'll dip those cattle and be friendly about it."

Peters' answer was to shove his spur into his horse and pound off through the dark.

Glenn walked on to his room, undressed, and lay tossing in the darkness, struggling with the problem of Peters. But the next morning, when he'd dressed and come out to the breakfast table, he sensed that he might just as well have pounded his ear. For Doctor Crane was still sore and a crisis hung in the air.

Glenn ate in silence and went quickly out to the barn. Maybe things would blow over—maybe the work at the hospital would smother last night's troubles with its demands.

Doctor Crane followed Glenn out to the barn. He

came in beside the roan, two vertical lines between his frosty gray eyes as he picked up Sky's healed foot.

"Nice heal," he said. "Good job of shoeing." He looked up and met Glenn's eyes, and in his own were the words, "But it's wasted."

"Thanks to Jensen," Glenn answered.

"No thanks to anybody," Doctor Crane added crisply.

Glenn flushed.

A silence settled over the barn. Only the flutter of pigeon wings in the rafters and the soft sigh of an early fall wind around the end of the barn came to warn Glenn.

The next instant, Doctor Crane said, "I'm going out to Harmon's ranch, Glenn. Their mare, Estrellita, has foaled. They want me to look the colt over—and the mare."

Doctor Crane paused, then with a look at Sky and another at Glenn added, "I want to take you with me. I want to show you Rocket, Des Harmon's wild palomino."

A real horse, Glenn told himself. That's what he wants to show me. A chance to get rid of Sky and get one like him if I want to hold my job here.

Aloud, he said, "Thanks, Doctor, I'd like that."

Doctor Crane went for his bag and in five minutes they were out on the graveled highway, going across the bridge of the St. Mary's, then turning eastward toward the line of blue Milk Ridge hills.

After ten miles they pulled into the ranch yard of the *Double Anchor*. It lay at the base of the ridge, a cluster of red and white buildings, with meadows stretching off toward a creek.

Mrs. Harmon came out, with little brown-eyed Janet, sharp as a cricket, and lugging her dog dressed in baby clothes.

Des greeted them and, after a moment, he and Harry led the way down to the barn and the new colt. "Dad's gone out with the fleet," he explained.

Glenn stepped across the sill and into the barn.

"Whew!" came to his lips. For from a box stall to the left came the soft nicker of a stallion, and above the stall, the shape of his head.

Doctor Crane paused, watching Glenn's eyes take in the magnificent golden horse before him.

"Wonderful animal," he said, with pointed quiet.

Glenn knew that he wanted him to see the difference between Sky and Rocket. He tried, too.

Carefully, he let his eyes go over the small beautiful head of the wild range stallion, telling himself, "He's really great." But then, he felt his lips add, "For Des." And within him came the knowledge that for him there was only Sky.

"Notice the breadth between the eyes," the doctor pointed out. "And the eyes themselves, so clear and full of fire, yet not mean."

Glenn gulped.

The doctor was giving it to him straight. He was showing him what to expect in a horse and, by inference, telling him, "Your roan's got none of these things."

Doctor Crane move down to Estrellita's stall where a sorrel mare stood beside a spindle-legged, newborn colt. Its nose butted at the mother's udder with impatient hunger.

With slow methodical hands the doctor examined the colt.

"Another Rocket, Des and Harry," he said at length. "Sure as you're born. Your father will be pleased."

"So will Hawkins down at the bank," Janet piped. "But he should worry, the old miser. We're selling colts as fast as we can raise 'em, clean down into California."

"Janet!" exclaimed Mrs. Harmon.

Glenn could only stand and listen, his thoughts a blur. Was he through with his job?"

It seemed so in the way the doctor closed the conversation and climbed back into the Dodge. It became more evident as they drove back toward Cardston, for at an intersection, Doctor Crane turned the car left.

"We'll drive out through Peters' range going back," he said.

Glenn, flushing, nodded.

The car moved along between the fenced lands of the grizzled rancher. White-faced cows with the *Rolling R* raised their heads to stare with soft eyes at the passing car.

Sleek, fat three-year-old steers, soon to be shipped from Cutbank, Montana, to the Chicago market, hooked each other's bodies with spread horns, or ran tail up before the exhaust of the speeding car.

Glenn did not speak.

Doctor Crane left no doubt in his mind as to what he was doing, as he guided the car along the country road.

"The Dominion Government sent me out here to clean up this cattle mange," he said, swinging the wheel to miss a rock in the road. "It's my responsibility, and will need all my time."

"Without a wild roan to hinder," Glenn whispered to himself, "or a bull-headed assistant who insists on hanging on to him."

"Yes," he said aloud. "It's going to be tough."

"If I fail, there'll be another man crowding me out," Doctor Crane carefully pointed out.

Glenn nodded.

The doctor turned to him.

"I'll need help, too. The right kind of help from my assistant; yes, without any distractions."

"Like an outlaw," Glenn breathed at length.

The doctor looked Glenn full in the face.

"Right!" he agreed.

In silence, then, the two rode along until, in the distance, the sprawling town of Cardston loomed. They clattered across the bridge, rode the two extra miles, and turned into the yard.

Stopping the car, Doctor Crane got out, reaching for his little black bag. For a second he stood there, waiting.

Glenn knew he wanted to hear, "I'll get rid of the roan, Doctor." But his lips wouldn't say the words. He kept feeling Sky's nose along his cheek that night down in the river bottom.

"I'm sorry, Doctor," he said. "But I can't give up Sky."

"As you wish," Doctor Crane's voice snapped. "Come into the office and I'll give you your time."

Ten minutes later Glenn came out of the hospital, folding a blue check in his trembling hands. Well, he was free, he told himself. But he felt as bound around and fenced in as a skim-milk calf in a yard.

"I'll get a haircut," he breathed, and turned toward town. "And a shave."

The chair hedged him in. He wanted to jump out of it, slam the steaming towel to the floor, and get away.

"Hear about that Barnes kid getting canned, up at the hospital?" a voice drawled. The man was climbing into the next chair. "Wonder what he'll do now—him and that roan he keeps penned up there in the barn?"

"I wonder?" Glenn whispered. A steam towel hid his face. A trembling seized him. He'd been working hard with things he liked: the yippy fox terrier with the torn lip, the big Chesapeake that must get well for Benton's hunting season.

Glenn thought he couldn't lie in the chair another minute. The thought of tomorrow without his job at the hospital came with crushing force.

"Boy," he whispered, squirming, "much more of this and I'll be an outlaw, too."

He tried the whispered words again, and again his trembling became violent. He couldn't stand the thought that flashed through his mind.

"Sky," he whispered, and sat up spilling the steaming towel to his lap. "Sky, I know now what's wrong with you."

Leaping from the chair, he flung a dollar bill at the barber, then fled from the shop and up the hill to the barn.

Opening the door, he moved softly over to the roan's stall.

"Well, Sky," he said gently, "you're all caged in

here, aren't you?" Running his hand along that silken-muscled back, he stood close to the roan, looking deep into those restless, caged eyes. "Boy, oh, boy, no wonder you're an outlaw!"

With swift hands he untied the roan and led him to the corral. On swift feet he brought out the saddle and saddled the roan.

He mounted, cheeking the horse so that he wouldn't kick him, taking a firm hold on the hackamore rope so that Sky wouldn't go over backward on him. Then, set deep in the saddle, he turned the roan loose.

Sky's bawling brought out half the town.

The dust rose from the corral like a fine mist.

"Look's like a fire at Doc's," said the farmer, who had first picked Glenn up from his ranch three miles distant.

Glenn rode the roan to a standstill.

He sat in the saddle, fighting, breathing hard, taking the jolts with stars shooting through his head. But always there was joy underneath, and his unspoken words, "Go to it, Sky. I know how you felt cooped up there in the barn."

At length, with the horse a-lather, and the doctor's eyes peering through the corral planks, Glenn yelled, "Open the gate!"

Law-and-Order opened it.

Horse and rider swept through and out to the plains.

It was dark when Glenn came back to the hospital. He rode up to the back door and called. Barbara came out, then Doctor Crane, a taller and thinner shadow by the dim light of the back porch.

It was touch and go for a moment, with the doctor's face set with his determination not to take Glenn back. But suddenly he looked at Sky rubbing his muzzle along his foreleg, shaking his head to get to the barn, like any saddle horse who'd been on a long ride and wanted to get to his stall.

The wind came dancing around the corner of the house, running soothing fingers through his thinning hair. It might have been Barbara's fingers or Joan's, his wife who had been dead for so many years.

"I—I see you've got yourself a saddle horse, Glenn," he said huskily.

Glenn, because those weren't the right words, waited.

"You—you could use him on the job," Doctor Crane groped for the words to explain that he wished Glenn back.

Glenn shifted his weight in the saddle.

"I could, Doctor," he said. "Because Sky's not only a saddle horse. He's a work horse. He can't stand being shut up or idle. He's a horse who's got to work hard every day, all day, doing things he likes, or else he gets tough."

Suddenly on the night air came the long whistle of a freight train coming across the river bridge toward Cardston. It was a long train of stock cars, loaded.

Doctor Crane's eyes met Glenn's.

"Tough—that's good," he said dryly. "For here comes Peters with his cows."

13. Midnight Herd

Larry Parks met Glenn the next morning at the Canadian Pacific Railway stockyards gate.

"You thought the train rolling in last night was Peters' Calgary cattle," he said, smoothing his sorrel's mane, then letting his gloved hand go down along his silvered martingale.

Glenn had to admit that was true. But staring at Larry's smooth blond face and laughing eyes, he thought, If I could only get Larry on my side of this mange fight. Maybe he could swing Peters our way, too.

"Yeah," he admitted, dismounting from Sky to stare at the long string of empty stock cars.

"Well, they were sheep for the Y outfit on Boundary Creek," Larry explained. His eyes grew sober and he moved his sorrel closer to Glenn. "Peters isn't shipping his stuff in," he explained. "He's trailing them."

"Oh," Glenn said, and waited. That meant Peters would have to bring them through Macleod ford. He'd probably do it at night. Take them across the Old Man River, then up across the reservation to the *Rolling R* on the quiet.

Larry leaned down to Glenn.

"Yeah," he said. He's trailing them. And he left

word for you and Doctor Crane to lay off. He thinks
you both are a couple of pill pushers and that you'd
better stick around the hospital and forget this mange
clean-up."

Glenn leaned against the big plank gate of the corral and let his eyes go out south and west to the cool
snowbanked Rockies. Tiny wisps of white clouds
flitted across the peaks and out over the prairie like
school children let out for a vacation.

He drew in his breath. This was a great country. It
would be the place to spend the rest of his life in, if
he got set. And the way to get set was to be friends
with men like Peters.

"Oh, that's what he thinks, is it?" he said softly.

Suddenly he leaned close to Larry.

"Larry," he said gently, "why don't you come in
out of the rain? You're going to have to, eventually.
Why don't you do it now by helping me get Peters
to see things our way?"

"Me, I like the rain," Larry said, straightening.
"Two hundred a month with time off for the Madison
Square Garden rodeo in the fall. A super string of
horses to ride and a good boss. Well, I got to get a-
long."

He turned his sorrel.

Glenn couldn't believe that Larry was so sure. He
must know that mange could be eradicated.

He mounted Sky and rode close to Larry. But before he could speak, Larry let him have it.

"I wasn't going to tell you this, Glenn," he said,
"but I see you're dead set on stopping Peters. Well,
you'd better not, see? He's bringing those dogies a-

cross the river at Macleod and he doesn't want any young squirt to get in his way, see?"

"But—" Glenn objected.

"No buts," Larry said. "Those cattle will be cagey. They'll be hard enough to shove across that ford without interference. Keep out, that's all. That's from Peters."

Before Glenn could stop him, Larry swung his big sorrel and moved off east. As he rode, the morning sunlight caught at the silver mounting on his saddle and martingale. It sent flicks of warning light back into Glenn's eyes.

Glenn moved Sky down the street toward the hospital, little puffs of dust rising under the roan's feet as he walked along. So that was the lay of the land. Peters was really handing it to them, take it or leave it, but stay clear.

He put Sky into his stall and, getting breakfast, walked into the hospital for the day's work. But working doggedly as he did, fixing up Rory, the big Chesapeake, for the day, and the second yippy fox terrier letting all the dogs out into their runs, Glenn knew that he'd have to go to meet Peters at the Old Man River ford.

Doctor Crane thought so too, when Glenn explained about the stock cars being a load of sheep. He sat in his office chair, looking up at Glenn with silent lips and snapping gray eyes.

"We won't back down," he said tersely. "The Indians are watching Peters and me. They'll soon begin to say, 'Peters no dip. Me no dip.'"

Glenn nodded.

"Just let Ottawa get a hint of Indian trouble and I'"

be sent for fast," Doctor Crane said, his fist pounding the desk. "I'll be asked to fly back and do some explaining."

Glenn didn't want Doctor Crane out of the country right now. What if he should have to go just about dipping time, when the fight with Peters reached its peak?

"The way to get around that is to head Peters off at the ford," Glenn said.

Doctor Crane nodded.

For a swift moment, the doctor and Glenn faced each other in the little office. As always to Glenn the smell of carbolic, the clatter of dogs barking, and the air of cleanliness of the place sent his pulse racing.

It would be worth a lot to win out here. Worth even the danger of facing up to Land Peters there in the dark of the night at Old Man River ford.

"Well," the doctor said, with sudden sharpness. "What are you waiting for, Glenn?"

Glenn felt his nerves tighten. They both knew what lay ahead, and how much depended on the outcome of it.

"I—I don't know," he said. But he did know. It was like riding into the strange waters of a swirling river, this riding to meet Peters. One minute you'd be on solid footing, the next, plunged under water with a treacherous slip-off of the river bed.

He straightened, then, knowing that he'd have to ride into it, come what may. He'd have to ride to win, too.

"I'll see Abbie and Luce," he said. "They will need money."

Glenn had earned one hundred and eighty dollars

now. Could it be possible he had been here two months? And that things could get as snarled up in that length of time?

"I'll go by the bank," he said. "Get my check changed to money, half for me and half for Luce."

"Half for Luce to blow on some invention," Doctor Crane snorted. "You'll be lucky if he doesn't get yours too."

Glenn thought of Luce and his heart skipped a beat. He'd surely be glad to see him again, and the doctor was so wrong about him.

"Oh, no," he said. "Luce is smart, and square. He wouldn't take my share, and he'll get hold of something that will run into big business some day, you'll see."

Doctor Crane's dry laugh answered him, then died before the solemn tone of his voice as he rose to take Glenn's hand.

"So long, and good luck. You'll need it," he said.

Glenn paused. The silence in the room seemed to thicken like a drying mudhole. He could almost hear the dull thud of cattle marching in the pitch darkness. Hear the wild shouts of *Rolling R* punchers urging the cattle toward Old Man River ford, marked by a huge cottonwood tree. See Peters, stiff and burly in his saddle, waiting for him to ride up.

"So long," Glenn managed, turning to walk from the room and toward the house. He'd throw a few things in a bedroll to tie behind his saddle.

In ten minutes, with Barbara waving from the kitchen window, Glenn walked toward the barn and Sky.

Law-and-Order Clements came from his house across the street and into the barn quietly, his solemn eyes on Glenn tying his roll. "I heard Larry telling about you going to stop Peters at the ford," he said. "But you'd better lay off. You won't get Peters to quit dumping his cattle loose without dipping them."

Glenn went on fixing to go. He had to admit that Ricky might be right.

"You don't think so?" he asked softly.

"No, I don't," Ricky shook his head. "Peters is smart and smooth. He's had his own way on this range ever since he was born."

Glenn finished tying the bedroll, then led Sky to the yard outside the barn door, with hands that tried to stay steady.

A stiff wind blew from the west. It was late afternoon. He could just make it to Standoff and spend the night. The next day he'd make it to the *Shoestring*, and—his thoughts broke off before the prospect ahead.

"You ought to stay here," Ricky said, hauling out the piece of torn mackinaw cloth he carried. Looking around to see that no one was near, he added softly, "This piece of cloth matched the coat of a big guy who watched you ride Sky the night he went so wild. I was standin' near him. I heard him say, 'I'll take him for the rodeo circuit now.'"

Glenn took hold of the cloth that matched the piece he carried. Again came that awful panic that he'd finally lose Sky to his real owner.

"Where is he now, Ricky?" he asked.

"He's skipped town. I didn't more'n catch a glimpse of him. But one of my gang heard him say he was comin' back—for the outlaw."

Glenn still held the cloth, figuring. But a slammed door at the hospital brought him back to the present.

"I'll keep watch, Ricky," he said. "But now, I've got to ride."

Slipping Sky's reins around that big muscular neck, Glenn mounted his saddle and gently touched the roan's sleek sides.

The big roan, with catlike grace, and a ground-eating running walk, moved out of the yard, down by the bank for a moment, then with Glenn in the saddle on out across the prairie toward Macleod.

The wind slapped at Glenn as he rode, as though to veer him to the east, anywhere but on to the Old Man River ford and Peters.

He held to his course.

The clouds, fleecy this morning, turned dark and large, spreading out to throw shadows of doubt a-round Glenn.

He shoved Sky all the harder.

At twilight, he crossed the bridge over the Belly River. He would have gone on for another ten miles to a bend in the river where he'd throw his bedroll, but Stanley, little and bald and worried, rode out from the agency to stop Glenn in the road.

Around him, forming a half circle, their "paint" ponies guided by a single throng of buckskin under the jaw, moved half a score of Blood Indian cattle owners.

"Little Snake warned us you were coming," Stanley began, shifting in his saddle. "We don't want trouble out here on the range. We want to be left alone as we've always been."

Glenn pulled Sky to face the scattered buildings

of Standoff: the long low shed of the storehouse, Stanley's house on the bank of the smooth river flowing past.

He turned his eyes back to Little Snake, lean and impassive on his pinto, to Ghost Chest, fat and stolid next to him, and to John Three Persons, cattle owner on the St. Mary's. If he could only get them on his side, then they could all ride down on Peters.

"Me no want trouble," he told the silent red riders.

"Ugh!" Little Snake grunted.

"Then you ride back to Cardston," Three Persons said, picking the words stolidly from his throat. "You leave us dip as Peters dips."

Glenn rode close to Three Persons. He looked square into his eyes.

"How you like it we dip once good. Once heap good, twice, like Great White Father in Ottawa want?"

He paused.

Silent angry looks passed round the Indians. They seemed to sit like graven statues of resentment.

"Then we dip no more," Glenn threw at them. "Mange gone, mistapoot!" He swung his arm in dramatic gesture. "Gone like coyote up coulee, who not come back."

For a second it looked as though Glenn had won.

He sat silent, not daring to breathe, while the picture of himself and these Indians riding to meet Peters filled his mind. Peters wouldn't dare be a standout then.

He saw Little Snake's bronze face relax. Three Person's burly hand dropped to his fat leg with fingers opened.

Then Ghost Chest spoke.

"Mange is not like coyote sneaking up draw. Mange is like gopher. He is everywhere. He goes in hole here. He comes out there. He is as the grass of the hills in numbers."

Ghost Chest's hand moved toward the hills dotted with gopher holes and covered with grass.

Glenn opened his mouth to speak.

Three Person's answer held him silent.

"Yes, if boy say mange is like coyote who not come back, he say lie."

Glenn knew it was useless to argue with the Indians. He turned beseeching eyes to Stanley. But Stanley had plenty to do in his job, to give out food to Indians on "treaty day," to keep track of the herds of cattle, and to keep the Indians good natured.

"I'm sorry, Glenn," he said. "These men own their own cattle. They have the say."

Glenn took a deep breath. Well, he had tried.

"Three Person's," he said, with more courage than he felt, "white boy no lie about mange. White Doctor no lie either. You dip this fall."

"Peters dip, too?" Little Snake grunted suddenly and in utter disbelief.

Glenn drew a second deep breath. He was really in it. His mind went out to the bank of the Old Man and the night and cattle surging down to the water. Cattle that had to be held close-confined until dipping time.

"Peters dip too," he nodded. "I ride to make him."

Glenn could feel the force of these Indians banded against him; their unbelief in him, a boy.

It seemed they would ride beside him, forming a V that would turn him back.

He picked up his reins.

Little Snake moved his pinto forward.

Three Persons moved his black and white to block him, followed by Ghost Chest on his red and white cayuse.

"Ugh! No go!" They grunted in unison, crowding in.

"Sky!" Glenn breathed sharply, loosening his reins.

The big roan's powerful body moved forward. For a moment his body seemed merged with the Indian ponies.

Then he gave a quick lunge.

The Indians swayed apart and Sky and Glenn moved on with the force of an explosion.

Putting spurs to the roan, Glenn left the Indians behind in a sudden wild rush for freedom.

For half a mile, fearing pursuit, he let Sky have his head. The big roan, as though sensing struggle, slipped effortlessly along the river toward the *Shoe-string*.

But then Glenn reined him in and, turning toward the river, followed its winding course at lessened speed.

Stopping beside the swirling current, Glenn threw himself from the saddle and to the edge of the stream. Drinking, he could hear Sky's muzzle downstream sucking in the cooling water.

When his thirst was quenched, Glenn stood beside his big roan, his hand along his neck, his thoughts on what had just happened with the Indians and Stanley. He was really in it now. He had to stop Peters, or the whole Blood tribe would follow his lead and there would be plenty of trouble.

He loosened his hand on Sky's neck.

The roan pawed the ground and shook his head.

Glenn studied the powerful horse, still fresh after twenty miles of road.

"So, you want to go on?" he whispered.

Sky tossed his head.

Glenn knew that he should not let Sky overdo. He should rest and graze. "Okay," he said, "but first, we'll eat."

Slipping the bridle from Sky's head, he let him graze on the tender grass along the riverbank, while he hauled out Barbara's bacon and egg sandwiches.

He ate, oblivious of the soft prairie night. The moon rode high and silvery in a sky dotted with fleecy clouds. Off on a bluff, a lone coyote sent his chattering cry downwind to him.

At length, having finished his lunch, Glenn stood up. He led Sky to the river for another drink, then rebridling him, pressed north.

Another time he would have enjoyed the roan's swift gait, the sweet way his legs moved, the muscular beauty of his neck, his flowing black mane tossed by the wind. Now he settled deeper in his saddle, urging the horse on toward the *Shoestring*, and the ford beyond where Peters would cross.

The moon rose higher. Glenn, listening to the soft swish of Sky's feet on the grass, and taking his bearings, guessed it must be around ten o'clock.

On and on he rode through the soft starlit night.

A second coyote barked sharply off to the left.

Another, close by, answered.

Glenn pushed on and, at a time he guessed must be around twelve, reached the turnoff in the road that led up river to the *Shoestring*. He hoped he'd be in time.

Glenn, without pausing a moment, pushed Sky up this trail to the little board house standing on the edge of the river bluff.

For a moment, at the edge of the porch, Glenn stared out across the bluff, past the barn, past Roy H's mound of dirt to the ford beyond.

Peters hadn't come yet.

Glenn's spirits lifted. He might meet Peters at the river and come to an agreement with him, when he did show up with his herd.

Glenn slid from his saddle to the porch.

The house was in total darkness, the windows like black staring eyes peering at him.

Glenn considered riding on down to the ford without waking them, but decided against it. He had money for Luce, and besides, he wanted to see them, even if for just a moment.

Stepping to the pine door, he knocked softly and called, "Anybody live here?"

Voices came to him, Abbie's clear, and Luce's bumbling like a bear's.

A light flickered on, went out, then went on again.

Then Luce was at the door, big as ever, words rumbling from his lips, his moist hand clasping Glenn's. Behind him, in her brown robe, her hair braided in a single smooth braid down her thin back, stood Abbie.

Even now, clasping him to her, Glenn smelled the cleanness of soap on her skin, and her kiss on his cheek was as cool and sweet as wind off a lake.

New courage flowed through him. He could count on their strength and backing for the task ahead.

"Hello, Glenn, glad to see you. Sure thought you'd gone away and forgotten us. We'll build up a fire and eat. Bet you're hungry," Luce talked. It sounded so natural.

Glenn would have liked to move inside. There was so much to tell; so much to talk over.

But as his foot stepped over the sill, from down river beside the trail came the low bawl of cattle.

For a second, standing there listening, Glenn's courage failed him. The cattle's low bellowing, the tramp of their hoofs across the grass, the wild shouts of the punchers, filled him with doubt as to what he could do.

Peters was there, he knew, silent, seated low in his saddle, leading the herd with no fuss, saying by his silent manner, "This is my business. I'm trailing these cattle across the reserve and cutting them loose on the *Rolling R* undipped. What are you going to do about it?"

But Glenn felt Abbie's firm hand on his arm, and turning, saw a light in her gray eyes.

"They're trailing cattle," Luce said. "They're Peters cattle. I heard all about it."

Glenn saw by Abbie's eyes that she had heard, too. She knew why the cattle were there, and why he was here as well.

Glenn waited for her lips to move, but no word came from them.

The cattle moved closer. Glenn guessed they must be within a quarter of a mile of the lone cottonwood that marked the entrance to the ford.

Looking out across the silver ribbon of water that was the river, he could make out the moving shape of the cattle, like a big black cloud floating across the land.

Then Abbie's lips did move, and a slight shove came from her hand. "Go on, Glenn," she said flatly. "Meet Peters, and don't back down."

Glenn was to remember the touch of her hand, and the strength of her voice through the trying days ahead.

Silently, not smiling at Luce's, "Yeah, go on, Glenn, don't take no sass from that Peters," Glenn handed the one hundred and eighty dollars he'd gotten at the bank to Luce, saying, "Half of this is yours, Luce. But you keep mine too." Then he mounted Sky.

He couldn't fail now. Not with Abbie's voice backing him. Not with the future of ranching here in southern Alberta and Doctor Crane's job, and his own life ahead at stake.

He tried, turning toward the river, to speak to Abbie and Luce. Words stuck in his throat. He could only put the spur gently to Sky's sleek sides and move swiftly toward the sound of the midnight herd.

14. Strange Accident

As GLENN reached the wooded river bottom and threaded Sky silently along the path leading to the trailing cattle, he was up against one of the major turning points in his life. Ahead, sitting his wild bay, leading the cattle, rode Peters—the man Glenn had to bring over to his way of thinking and keep as a friend while doing it.

A tautness filled Glenn, but with it came a bit of hope. Surely he could make Peters come across. The man had sense, didn't he?

Sky under him, solid, moving with effortless ease, contributed to Glenn's hope of winning out.

Settling himself deeper in his worn saddle, Glenn pushed his roan to the river's edge. The swirling water, silvery in the moonlight, hurried past him, suggesting speed. The whispering cottonwoods above him, seemed to say, "It's your time, Glenn."

He squared his shoulders and, touching Sky's sides with his spurs, pushed the roan out into the swirling water. The horse waded in up to his belly, to his flanks, then suddenly dropped off into deep water and struck out for the lone cottonwood on the other shore.

Peters was waiting for him as Glenn reached the

other side. He did not speak, as horse and rider came dripping from the ford.

In silence, then, the two riders swung their mounts, riding back perhaps a hundred yards to the leaders of the herd. There, they swung about, guiding the lead cattle down to the water's edge.

The main herd behind them pressed silently on. It was necessary to start the leaders across.

Peters thrust forward, his bay shoving the lead steers toward the water. Glenn brought up Sky's big roan body to his support.

The leaders sheared off, refusing to take to the water. The cattle began milling.

Riders came up to swarm into them, trying to force the band across. It seemed futile.

The small lead bunch eluded the riders, dodging back into the main herd that pressed closer.

Peters took down his rope to toss it for a lead steer's horns. He missed.

Glenn took down his. It wouldn't do any harm to help out right here. It would give him a chance to bargain with Peters.

Shoving Sky forward, he singled out a brockle-faced steer with wide flowing horns. His rope sang out, descending over the steer's horns. Glenn jerked it taut, took his dallies around his saddle horn and moved Sky toward the ford.

The steer bellowed. He cat-walked, squirming and bawling, jumped sideways, then set his feet.

Glenn sat deep in his saddle, speaking to Sky.

The big roan seemed to enjoy his work. He crouched low under the straining rope. With the creak of the saddle in his ears, he dug his hoofs into the soft ground and moved toward the water.

The steer bawled. He shoved deep into the ground, then, with a roar, shot forward.

They reached the river and went into it.

From the tail of his eye, Glenn caught sight of the band of steers following the leader. He pushed Sky deeper into the river. The water rose to his stirrups, then to the roan's withers. Glenn raised his legs around the saddle horn. A steer was swimming now, and behind him the herd was coming willingly into the water.

A sort of joy sang through Glenn, with Sky swimming across the wide river. He guessed Peters wouldn't think he was only a pill pusher now. The beauty and wildness of the scene filled him with pleasure and hope for what lay ahead.

Surely Peters would meet him on some kind of mutual deal now?

Cattle around him swam for the nearing shore. They swam in groups, their heads and horns showing along the silvery water. Little calves, beside their mothers, swam with short strokes of their flailing legs.

Swiftly Glenn reached the bank and then was out.

The steer had reached the bank and was climbing dripping from the water.

Glenn ran Sky along the steer's side and, reaching down, put three fingers under the loop, singing it through the honda. In seconds, the steer was free of the rope and pushing on, with the herd following.

Glenn swung to one side, waiting, coiling his stiff rope.

Peters rode up, and another puncher came from the

river. Peters motioned the other puncher to take his place and lead the herd.

He swung to one side facing Glenn.

Glenn caught his breath. On Peters' face he read only determination, and knew this was not the time to argue with the rancher. With studied silence he bent to strap his rope on his saddle tree, hearing the slow tread of the herd passing by, headed for the reservation and the *Rolling R*.

Peters said, "Nice job you did there, Glenn."

"Thanks," he said and waited.

"I could use you on the *Rolling R*," Peters said, trying to quiet his bay which had suddenly gone mean.

"You could work up to be foreman," Peters said. "I'm a bachelor"—he paused, then went on with quiet suggestion—"the *Rolling R* has to go on after I cash in."

Glenn still waited. No mention of dipping.

At length he knew there wouldn't be. Peters had set his head.

Then Glenn got as stubborn as Peters. Along with the courage that was oozing from him, and the knowledge that what had seemed so easy was getting more difficult all the time, came a burning rage within him.

Who was Peters to say what should be done here on the range?

"I have a job, Mr. Peters," he said, suddenly swinging in his saddle to face the short, rugged cowman. "That's why I'm here tonight. To tell you that you're going to dip these cattle before kicking them loose on the *Rolling R*."

Peters was just able to keep his bay from bolting.

Bringing the big mean, shifty horse back to face Glenn, Peters eyed the boy in stolid silence.

"You've never given the doctor a fair break," Glenn argued. "Never rounded up all your cattle, and I mean all, at each dipping. If you'd try it once, you'd be surprised at the results."

Peters fought his moon-eyed bay back once more. The horse had defective vision, seeing shadows where there were none.

Peters clamped his jaws tight. His eyes were tired from the day's trail; his lips, dry with dust, tightened. A dull red climbed his neck.

"I've said it a hundred times, and I say it again: so long as there are cattle on the range there will be mange."

He swung his horse to ride away.

Glenn could not believe he had lost with Peters. Riding through the trees toward the ford, it had seemed so sure. When Abbie had touched his arm, he had thought he couldn't lose. And now the Indians wouldn't dip either. Doctor Crane would be called back to Ottawa; would lose his job.

Glenn tightened his reins to follow Peters, then let them drop.

"No use," his dry lips whispered.

All at once, with Peters but a few feet distant, a tumbleweed came rolling by. It snarled in the feet of the bay. It sent the horse high, in a rearing frantic struggle to free his legs of it.

The movement angered Peters, and it caught him off guard.

His body swung sideways, his hands clutched for

the saddle horn and missed, and the solid man went down just as the bay started to bolt.

Glenn expected to see Peters' body fall to the grass. It would be simple to round up his horse.

Peters did not fall to the grass. His shoulders hit the ground, but his foot hung from the stirrup of the frightened bay that started running in a circle, moon eyes on the fallen, dragging man.

Glenn caught his breath. In seconds, the bay would break from the circle and run. Fear-crazed he would kick the trailing Peters to ribbons with his sharp hoofs.

For what seemed an hour, but must have been seconds, Glenn sat Sky, immovable, feeling unable to act. Suddenly a voice within him prompted, "Your rope."

His hands flew to it, made a loop with the smooth speed of long practice.

"Throw it," the voice urged. "Before it's too late. Catch the bay, draw him down, choke off his wind."

But it was too late already. The bay had turned to run, dragging the helpless rancher head down across the grass.

The bay was going. He was fast and deadly wild.

Glenn flung out his loop.

It sang out and out and out. But was the bay beyond it?

Glenn uttered a groan. Was the rope slacking off along the bay's neck, missing his sleek wild head? But now, the rope tautened.

With a cry, Glenn took his dallies, tightened his reins, swung Sky to face the fleeing bay, and waited for the impact.

The bay reached the end of the rope. The loop

tightened. It sang through the honda. It closed on the wild fighting neck of the bay and, under the impact, flung him to the ground.

Moving with feline speed, Glenn slipped from his saddle. By the time the bay was fighting to his feet, Glenn's hands had released the unconscious Peters' boot from the stirrup.

The bay clambered up and stood snorting close by.

Peters lay where he had fallen, quiet, his sunburned face turned to the sky.

Glenn knelt beside the cowman.

He knew that he had Peters cold, if he wanted to play it that way. Peters was all man. He'd come out of this and say, "Okay, Glenn, you saved my life. I'll give in."

Then a woman's voice at his side put into words what Glenn had just decided for himself.

"You can't take advantage of Peters just because you saved his life," she said, reading the struggle going on within him.

It was Abbie who must have been watching from her house and, seeing the accident in the moonlight, had come across to them there on the river knoll.

Glenn faced her. Peters was coming around. The rancher's lips moved in a groan.

"It's got to be of his own free will, Glenn," Abbie pleaded. "His consenting to dip correctly, I mean."

Glenn knew that she was right. He turned to look down at Peters, now breathing naturally, moving his hands, trying to speak. Then he looked back at Abbie.

She nodded her understanding.

"I'll clear out for Cardston and Doctor Crane," Glenn said.

"I'll see that Peters is looked after," Abbie promised.

Riding along toward Cardston, with Sky's hoofs swishing the grass in a dull throbbing pound, Glenn caught his breath. A sense of futility and doubt crept through him again.

Had he been a high-minded chump about Peters? He'd left it up to the rancher, and what would the grizzled cowman do? Would he come across?

15. Calamity

As GLENN rode down the main street of Cardston at ten o'clock the following night, he thrust off the forbidding silence of the street.

Intent on getting to Doctor Crane to tell of Peters' trailing the cattle and of his saving his life and his plan of bringing him into line, he reined Sky up the hill, whispering, "Come on, boy, only a little farther, just climb the hill to your stall."

What a horse! he thought. Eighty miles of road and a river crossed twice, with only two hours' rest grabbed shortly after leaving Abbie and Peters there on the knoll.

There was a light coming from Alan's double window as Glenn rode up to the barn, but Doctor Crane's house was dark.

Glenn's heart sank. He had hoped to tell the doctor at once.

He drew in his breath and, moving into the stall, slipped Sky's saddle from his tired back, fed him some hay, and bedded him down.

"I'll be out later to give you your oats and a drink of water," he said, feeling the roan's sweaty flank. "We don't want you to have a spell of colic."

Sky nickered softly, then plunged his head into the

hay, sending it flying. Glenn snapped off the light, left the barn and walked toward Alan's room.

Suddenly a swish of wings hovered around his head. A flat black body landed plump on his shoulder and a cold bill pressed against his cheek.

"Help! Murder!" the bird shrieked.

Glenn took the pet crow in his arms.

"Screamer, whatever are you doing here?" he asked. "You're Jim Starr's crow from down on the St. Mary's ranch."

Carrying the crow along toward Alan's room, he figured the bird must have been lured to freedom by a flock of wild crows, then set upon by them.

Opening the door to the hospital, with Screamer yelling, "Help! Murder! Get out!" Glenn poked his head into Alan's room.

He wanted to see the doctor right away. Maybe Alan would know where he was.

Alan lay on his cot, reading *Microbe Hunters* by Paul De Kruif. He raised questioning eyes that held a deep reserve in them, as though life had given him another knock that he'd had to absorb.

"Hello, thought you were staying till Sunday," he said, then let his voice trail off at what he saw in Glenn's eyes. "Oh," he said. Reaching for an old blotter, with Peck's Dog Food in big red letters on it, he marked his place in the book.

Glenn tried to keep his voice quiet. "How's things?" he asked. "And where is Doctor Crane?"

Alan shook his head. "Things aren't so good," he said, trying to speak easily, but with that something bothering him. "Rory, Benton's Chesapeake, may not pull through. He's developed pneumonia. Had to put a jacket on him to ease his pain in breathing."

"Help! Murder!" screeched Screamer.

Even above his urgency, Glenn couldn't help smiling. And Alan, as Glenn examined the pecked head of the bird, allowed a wispy smile to cross his sensitive lips. Then he added, "And the doctor isn't here."

Glenn all but dropped Screamer as he carried the bird into the treating room to wash his head, then put him in a cage for the night.

Coming back to Alan, he asked, "Not here, then where is he?"

Alan again picked up his book, seeming to want the conversation to end.

"Look, Glenn," he said, "you're done in. You're pale as a ghost. And about Doctor Crane, you'd better get it from Barbara." His eyes dropped to his book.

Glenn surveyed Alan's passive figure in silence for a moment. What went on here? Something had happened that Alan was having trouble absorbing. And Doctor Crane wasn't here.

"Okay, I'll see Barbara," Glenn said softly, and swinging around went out of the door and across the dark yard to the house. He decided he'd straighten out whatever it was that had hurt Alan. Alan was a right guy, and they'd finally be friends.

Barbara came up just as he stepped on the porch, coming from another of her numerous meetings.

"Glenn," she exclaimed, "I'm so glad you're here." Drawing him inside, she took one look at him, then flew to stir up the fire. "You're fagged," she went on. "And Dad's gone, been called to Ottawa. Ricky's mother is staying with me."

Glenn tried to edge a word in. But Barbara's voice went on, "Alan's angry, and in a way I don't blame him. But Dad said you'd be in charge here." Her voice dropped to a grave whisper. "He's left Peters for you to handle."

The frying pan clattered onto the stove, the frying ham and potatoes sizzled. Then with his face washed and his thick red hair combed down, Glenn sat down to eat and to study the situation.

Boy, was he in it now! Doctor Crane gone, Alan hurt and offended, and only he himself to decide how to handle this thing.

Glenn put things in his mouth and swallowed because he knew he must eat. There was too much ahead to play namby pamby and flirt with food.

When he had finished, he turned around in his chair. After a moment he got up to dry the dishes for Barbara. It made him feel better to keep moving, and it gave him a chance to tell her all about the cattle and Peters.

"Now, Barbara," he said, carefully drying a glass until he could see a drawn white face he supposed was his own in it, "what would you do?"

"Oh, it's all so confusing," Barbara said, pouring out the sudsy water.

"Yes, it is," he managed dully, and slipping into his windbreaker went out to the barn.

Alan came in to take a last look at the filly. Quietly, without a word to Glenn, fixing up Sky for the night, he went on tending the mare. Then, slipping softly toward the door, he would have gone out without speaking.

"Yes?" he said to Glenn's, "Oh, Alan, just a moment."

He came in to sit on a bale of hay and stare fixedly at Glenn through the whole of his story about Peters and the cattle.

When Glenn had finished, Alan rose quickly and walked toward the door once more.

"It's up to you, Glenn," he said. "You're in charge here. I'm staying strictly out of it." Once more he had withdrawn into himself.

Glenn felt sick inside. Why hadn't Doctor Crane left them in joint charge? Alan had seniority, and really had a right to be sore. But of course, as Barbara had pointed out, Alan wasn't a range man and he wouldn't know how to argue with a tough hombre like Peters.

"But you've an opinion?" Glenn probed.

Alan took a step back toward Glenn.

"There're two ways to handle it," he said. "You've got Peters over a barrel if you want to tell him you saved his life. All you have to say then is, 'What about it, Peters? Are you going to chintz out?' Then there's the other way, stay clear and wait for Peters to come across on his own." Alan turned and walked to the barn door, then turned again. "Take your choice, Glenn," he said, "in the next eleven days. But it's your choice, not mine, when you do."

He stepped across the sill and moved off into the dark.

And he had been so friendly for a while! Glenn would have liked to tell him that he, Glenn, didn't begin to know all Alan did about animals and hospital routine. Couldn't he see this range business was a special case? But no, better to go along and assume later that Alan understood it had no meaning, that Alan still came first.

"Eleven days," Glenn whispered, dumping a can of crushed oats into Sky's feed box. "Eleven days before dipping day."

The nearness of Sky probed him. The horse who'd have to work and work hard if he was to stay sweet tempered. The prospect of eleven days struck at him as though each day were a number springing from a calendar to his neck to weigh him down.

Suddenly Glenn flung the oat can back to its bin and, going toward the door, switched off the light and gained his room.

"I'll play it that Peters will come across," he decided, slipping from his clothes and under his comforter. "I'll play it that people do the right thing." Snuggling deeper under the covers he yawned and added, "And I'll work Sky until he cries 'Uncle,' teaching him tricks."

Glenn turned on his side and yawned again.

Work reached out and grabbed Glenn the next morning. It was the hard work of the hospital with its endless routine of feeding, dressing wounds, and caring for the animals.

Rory was no better, but lay breathing hard, in pain, his eyes blurred and half closed. There was Jim Starr to call and tell about his crow, and above all else there was the road to watch for some sight of Peters' coming.

But Peters did not come. There was no sign of the grizzled, silent rancher's body on his big bay riding in to alight at the hospital door, throughout the day or that evening.

Glenn finished supper, then went out to saddle Sky and lead him into the corral.

Alan, because he'd grown to like Sky, came with his accordion. Perching on the top pole of the corral, he said, "Let's go," and struck up the lively *Blue Danube*.

For an hour, two hours, Glenn worked with the big blue horse, teaching him to lift his feet high in a slow even pace. He knew better than to make Sky follow music, realizing that the music must always follow the horse. The trick was to get Sky to keep an even gait with high slow steps.

At length, the roan moved around the corral, forefeet stepping high, head up, his tail switching with pleasure.

But when he had finished, there had been no sign of the stubborn Peters.

"One day passed," Glenn said doggedly and led Sky into his stall.

Larry Parks came in. "Did you know that the Indians aren't going to fix their vat?" he needled.

"They will," Glenn said, with more confidence than he felt.

The next day was Sunday and Glenn, with the feeding over, dressed in his blue suit and went with Barbara to Sunday School.

As usual, Alan refused to go.

It made pink spots come into Barbara's cheeks, and kept her silent on the walk along the sidewalk to the little white-painted church with the steeple,

west of the hospital. "Doris, Alan's girl, wrote me
he'd act this way," she said.

Glenn, his eyes on the horizon, told her that Alan
was content as he was. Then with a dull feeling within, he went inside the church. The horizon had been
free of a rider.

With church out, Glenn saddled Sky and rode east
to the Milk River. There, under a bluff, he swam and
lay in the sun on a sandbank.

He thought he was through with worrying about
Peters for the day, until a bunch of *Rolling R* cows
came winding down the slope to drink.

Glenn sat up, with a hollow feeling inside him.
These were some of the cows Peters had trailed from
Calgary.

A rider appeared briefly on a bluff down river.

Glenn caught his breath.

"Peters!" he whispered.

But the rider, after a moment's study of Glenn and
Sky grazing close by, turned and faded from sight.

"It wasn't Peters," Glenn breathed. Slowly dressing, he rode Sky back to the hospital in dogged
silence.

It seemed but a moment until the next Sunday,
with only three days left for Peters to come across.

Glenn tramped into his room and peeled off his
clothes. He'd been for another swim, hoping vainly
that Peters might ride to him.

Glenn climbed into bed but couldn't sleep. He got
up and walked to the window, staring into the starlit
night.

Overhead the Milky Way made a white band of

stars across the sky. Flashes of heat lightning flickered over Ahern Glacier to the south and west over the Rockies.

Suddenly, Glenn's eyes riveted on a burly figure inching along the corral fence toward the barn. For a second, Glenn thought it might be Alan, but it was too heavy for him. Perhaps it was some stranger who had wandered off the streets and would go on past the barn to the opposite sidewalk. But no, he was heading for the barn. He had his hand on the barn door. He softly opened it.

On impulse, Glenn stuck his head out of his window, calling, "Hey, what do you want?"

The man's action was swift and planned. He turned, and, running low, keeping his face averted, slipped around the corner of the barn.

Glenn heard a boyish call of distress, then the sound of a horse's feet pounding into the night.

Glenn slipped through the window and ran barefooted to the barn and around the corner.

"Ricky!" he exclaimed.

Ricky Clements, the Law-and-Order man, with the wind knocked out of him, fought to his feet.

"I saw him close," he said. "He has a scar along his cheek. He has black mean eyes, and he's the guy who was looking through the corral bars that night you rode Sky."

"Yeah?" Glenn, followed by Ricky, moved around to flash on the barn light, then study the deep bootheel marks made in the soft dirt at the barn entrance.

"He's the same guy who's sayin' around town, 'The big roan's ready for rodeos,'" Ricky blurted.

Glenn felt sick. It look as though Sky's owner had

shown up. Balleau? But why didn't he come out in the open?

Glenn knew that he would try again for Sky, and in the same stealthy way. Moving across the sill, he walked in beside the frantic horse.

"Sky, Sky," Glenn soothed. "Take it easy, boy. He won't get you." But he wondered, studying the sprawling *C* brand on the roan's thigh, if he spoke the truth.

For an hour he worked around Sky, quieting him down, then at length, with a last slap at Sky's flank, he went out of the barn and to bed.

Monday passed, with no sign of Peters.

Tuesday passed. Still the horizon held no rider coming to Glenn.

Tuesday evening, his body taut with waiting, Glenn brought Sky out to the corral, saddled and ready for more tricks. Law-and-Order Clements and his pals ringed the corral's top pole. Alan came with his accordion, striking up the music.

Glenn mounted the big horse and started him around the corral in a high-stepping cakewalk that was beautiful to see. Every line of the big roan was a thing of flowing beauty.

Sky made the complete circle to Alan, then rearing to his hind legs walked on them for half a turn around the corral.

"It takes a strong back to do that." Law-and-Order's voice came with authority. "I read it in an article on horse training."

Glenn dropped the horse to four feet.

A fine dust rose from the ground.

He couldn't help looking off toward the main

street of town thinking that Peters, tight-lipped but fair, must surely come up to talk it over.

"He must do it," Glenn whispered. "He's that kind of man."

But no Peters came riding.

Glenn stood his horse there in the corral, and a fine sweat came out all over him. Had he been more than foolish? Should he ride down to Peters' ranch, even now, and say, "This is fine repayment for saving your life. What are you going to do about it?"

He passed a hand across his wet brow. It was a lot of responsibility, and why didn't Doctor Crane show up from Ottawa?

As he moved Sky to the gate he was tempted to say, "Open the gate, Law-and-Order, I'm riding." Could he still go to Peters and wring a deal out of him?

But at the gate, his hands on the latch, Glenn felt an obstinacy seize him, and a stubborn clinging to his original plan. No, sir, Peters could play this thing any way he pleased, but he wouldn't go to him. Abbie was right. He must wait Peters out. He rode the roan into the barn and unsaddled him.

"Tomorrow, Sky," he said, "we'll go swimming again. Down by the river we'll wait Peters out."

With more courage than he felt, Glenn slipped from the barn to his room and, flinging off his clothes, dived into bed.

He waited out Peters until it was Wednesday and Glenn was again flinging off his clothes, but this time for diving into the river.

Sky, big and blue as the sky above them, grazed,

unsaddled and dragging his hackamore rope, down the river bend.

Glenn could not feel the water. Everything about him was numb. His mind lay down river at Peters' ranch. For this was Wednesday; dipping day. The day that Peters must fix the vat and round up the cattle, all the cattle. He must send word to Stanley and the Indians that he was dipping and they would do the same. In Ottawa things would be straightened out and Crane would come back to supervise the dipping on the reserve.

Glenn dived again and swam across the river and back.

He crawled to the bank and stood, dripping wet and brown naked, listening for the sound of bellowing moving cattle.

No sound reached his ears.

The sun lay low across the slash of blue mountains to the west and south. A chill evening breeze sprang up, rustling the grass along the riverbank.

Still no sound of bawling cattle, no cries of punchers, no slap of ropes along "chaps," to tell of a roundup.

Then around the bend, entirely on their own, unchecked, not rounded up, came a band of *Rolling R* cows. Shivering and crawling into his clothes, Glenn knew then that he was licked. Peters wasn't going to come across. In a kind of dull rage, Glenn finished dressing.

Sky wasn't around. Glenn yanked his shirt over his head, and guessed the roan must have drifted down river. He'd have to go after him.

He clapped his Stetson on, deciding stormily that

he was a fine judge of human nature thinking Peters would come through. "He can do what he likes. I'm sticking to what I planned. I'm still waiting him out."

Hardly knowing where he was going, Glenn started walking along the river to get Sky. The horse must be around that next river bluff.

But suddenly across the sky line came a lone rider, moving slowly, then, at sight of Glenn, swinging to ride down to him.

"Peters," Glenn whispered, his belly taut. "Coming to crow over me."

He moved faster, away from the riding cowman. Let Peters come and gloat over him. It was okay. He'd guessed wrong, that was all. He'd ride Sky up and out of the country and get a job elsewhere.

Peters caught up with him and rode in front of Glenn, to head him off. Glenn had to stop.

Peters, stiff, burly, his deep-set eyes that could be so stubborn on Glenn, demanded, "What are you doing here? Don't you know you should be at the vat, testing the mixture, telling me to go and round up all my cows?"

Glenn tried to walk past him. If the stubborn old mule hadn't tumbled to what was right by now, he probably never would. He did not answer Peters.

"You figured I'd be man enough to come across on my own, that it?" Peters growled.

Glenn felt the explosion within him coming. He tried to head it off, but the words fairly leaped out of his mouth. "Check, Peters," he snapped out. "I guess that's what I did think." He made it around Peters' horse then and trudged doggedly along the brown grass.

Suddenly Peters spurred his bay and caught up with Glenn. His face, wind-burned and lined, broke into a thin smile. It was like the first crack in the sheet ice of Milk River in a spring thaw. He leaned down and held out a rope-burned hand.

"You figured right, then, Glenn. We'll be a day late, but I'm dipping thorough, and I'll see that the Indians do, too. Shake, Glenn."

Climbing the river bluff, with Peters gone, relief flooded Glenn. It was wonderful. He had made a friend of Peters for life. The future was rosy. It was like a view from a high bluff such as this, with all the world spread out smooth and brown and wonderful before one. Doctor Crane's job was safe. Alan would be made to understand, and he and Sky could go on working. Later, he'd go to Ames.

Glenn quickened his pace to reach the peak of the bluff.

Boy, would the roan like to hear of this! He'd tell him, and Sky, rubbing his head along his windbreaker, would understand.

But on reaching the bluff's top, Glenn drew up sharply. Sky wasn't in sight.

Glenn searched the slope to the river with darting eyes. He began to run down toward the river, then stopped short. Off across the river, four men rode, dragging a horse between them.

Glenn caught a flash of white across the captive horse's eyes. They had blindfolded Sky. It was the only way they could take him.

"Sky!" Glenn cried and began futilely running toward the swirling river. "Sky, come back." It was the scar-faced man and his gang, Glenn knew. He'd taken Sky. He'd throw him into rodeos again; make a killer horse of him once more.

Glenn ran to the river's edge.

The men moved from sight, dragging Sky. He faded into the dusk, a phantom horse at the end of a lariat. The swirling muddy water at Glenn's feet sucked and gurgled with a hopeless sound.

16. The Clue

GLENN had hitchhiked home that night; caught a ride with an old homesteader in a Ford from Del Bonita. Piling in beside the farmer with his saddle he had sat in slumped misery all the way to Cardston.

Once there, he had saddled Buck, against Alan's advice and Barbara's pleading, and had ridden all night. The next day he worked with Peters at the dipping vat. Word had gotten around and the grizzled old cowman would have looked sympathetic if he'd been able. The next night Glenn rode down through Browning, Cutbank, and as far east as the little oil town of Shelby. The next night he rode again but no sign of Sky met his anxious eyes. No forefoot hoofmark that would betray the whereabouts of the phantom roan.

Once, just across the Milk River, Glenn had picked up the rain-soaked trail—for it had rained hard, a three-day fall rain before the first snow. But once on the open prairie, the deep imprint of Sky's peculiar hoofmark had faded and then vanished completely.

Reluctantly Glenn turned Buck for home.

Each day that followed he rose at dawn, working doggedly, quietly, until suppertime, then went to his own room to lie and think and wonder if he had missed Sky's trail at some point in his search.

But one night, as he walked to his room, Barbara excitedly stopped him. Red spots glowed in her smooth cheeks and her blue eyes sparkled as she talked.

"I took your advice about Alan," she burst out. "I took it easy about urging him to come to meetings and waited. Then Doris wrote him to sing, and now, tonight, you're going to hear him."

Glenn's first impulse was to avoid it. But then he thought it might take his mind off Sky.

"Okay, Barbara." He nodded. "I'll take a shower and meet you there."

"Don't be late," Barbara cautioned. "It's going to be wonderful. Alan wouldn't come unless we got others to sing songs of their countries. Anna Larson's going to sing some Norwegian songs, little Eagle Feather's going to sing and do a war dance of the Bloods', then Alan's going to sing early songs of the slaves."

An hour later, Glenn walked inside of the little white-painted church and took a seat near the back of the hall. There was always a chance that Law-and-Order might come in, saying that Sky had come back home. Sky would come home, Glenn knew, if he could break loose from his captors.

But no Law-and-Order showed up. Glenn sat in dull misery, half listening to Barbara who, as president, opened the meeting.

A small Indian boy in a white fawn-skin suit and beaded moccasins moved soundlessly as a night wind to the platform and sang a monotonous chant of the

Blood Indians. Then to the beat of drums of two young tribesmen, he did a weaving war dance.

Applause filled the hall, then laughter, because no amount of coaxing would pry little Eagle Feather loose from his seat for an encore.

He sat clutching the bench, his face a dull brown mask, his jet-black braids bobbing to the shake of his head.

In the fading laughter, Anna Larson, who kept house for Leif and Big Chris Olson of Magrath, rose and walked to the platform, her braids shining in the light, her lithe body moving with effortless grace. Smoothing her white Hardanger lace apron, and adjusting her little red jacket, she sang an old Norwegian folk song. It was a song of the high rocky mountains of Norway: *Saetergjerten's Söndag, the Herd Girl's Sunday.*

Glenn couldn't help listening to her words describing the song: how the girls of Norway in early spring took the cattle to the hills to graze. There, living in chalets, high in the mountains, they stayed the summer through, making cheese and butter in the high cool country: to amuse themselves, and because they were often lonely, they sang.

"This song is of a girl on a Sunday morning," Anna's voice came distantly to Glenn. "She is lonely and wishes that summer would end so that she can go home to the valley and to her sweetheart."

Glenn sat trying to concentrate on Anna's song, which was really beautiful, and then the encore, *Kjôre Vatten og Kjöre Ve, Carry Water and Carry Wood.*

Taking the accordion from Anna's hands, Alan got up and took his seat on the stage.

At the first few notes from the accordion, Glenn felt he could hardly stand it. He sat clenching his hands through two old Negro songs of early slave days. Alan sang in a rich soft voice. He seemed happy and glad. He played another song and then told about his grandfather, a roustabout on the Mississippi river boat, *Golden Paddles*.

Glenn sat listening to it and the song that followed, a thing of low tones filled with the smell of the river, the gliding deadly water moccasins along its banks, and the moon over trees filled with Spanish moss. The soft crooning voices of the natives were there, then the story of *Golden Paddles*, its explosion, and the grandfather's narrow escape.

In the applause that followed, Glenn joined mechanically.

Then Alan suddenly drew the accordion to him and swung into the *Blue Danube*.

Glenn caught his breath: pictures of the big roan in the corral came to slip past his closed eyes. Memories of their wonderful times together learning to dance to this tune crowded into his head.

"Sky," he breathed, "where are you tonight?" With swift caution, he rose and slipped from the hall into the cool darkness of the night.

But even there the cool wind brought back pictures of Sky. The distant stars reminded him of the campfires of Indians along the Belly River, and of his rides there with the roan.

Glenn passed a shaking hand across his forehead

as he moved toward the hospital. He would have to keep on looking for Sky.

A week later, Doctor Crane, who had come home, put it into words: "You look unhappy, Glenn. After the way you won over Peters I owe you a great deal. Isn't there something I can do?"

"Guess I'll have to take a week off," Glenn said. "I'm sorry, with all you've got to report on to Ottawa, but I have to get my bearings."

Out on the reservation, riding toward the *Shoestring*, Glenn knew what he would do. He'd get his share of the money he had left with Luce and ride across the line for Sky. He would ride until he found some clue, then doggedly trace it down.

He reached home but, before he could more than kiss Abbie and shake Luce's hand, Luce had him walking toward the barn and across the sill into the tack room.

"I got her this time, Glenn," he panted, his voice high with excitement. "I got us the formula for a fortune, cold."

Apprehension tingled Glenn's spine like a tiny rivulet of ice water. His share of the money—what had Luce done with it?

He hadn't long to wait before knowing.

Reaching behind two sacks of oats, Luce brought out a brown-paper parcel, and opened it with trembling hands.

A green-covered can came first.

"Not that," Luce said in disgust. "That was just thrown in. It's a sample of a weed killer. The fellow gave me the formula and all rights, too. I've got it somewhere in my papers. But—" Moving to the barn door he tossed it into a moonlit patch of Canada thistle. "There, that settles that," he said, brushing his hands. "But now—" He came ambling back to Glenn like a big black bear. "Now for the beauty—the beauty!"

Before Glenn's somber eyes, he hauled from the brown-paper sack a thing of mysterious weights and paddles and springs. Luce's hands held it on a slant, and paddles went around and around.

"There she is," Luce exclaimed, his eyes shining into Glenn's. "The little old red and white fortune maker. The only genuine perpetual-motion machine in the world. And we own it, Glenn. I got it for just the amount of money you gave me."

Glenn's first reaction was to blow up at Luce. Taking his money that he'd wanted to use for hunting Sky! But the sight of the old man's face by the flickering light of his lantern squelched the hot words boiling up within him.

He took the paper Luce handed him. He smiled as Luce went on explaining. "We're partners, Glenn. Here, I fixed the papers up legal. You keep one and I keep one. Then, when the money rolls in, we'll have proof that we're a couple of pretty smart hombres, eh?"

Glenn stuffed the partnership paper in his pocket, while the memory came back to him of Luce's voice saying, "We're going to run the mowing machine, aren't we, Glenn?" That had been when Glenn was ten; but he'd never forgotten how Luce had always wanted to share and make him feel important.

He walked to the barn door, his heart swelling within him, a hard lump forming in his throat.

He put a hand on Luce's arm as the old man followed him, and stared up into the brilliant night sky. If Luce had bought six of those twinkling stars shining above him right now for that money, it was his right.

"Yes, sir," Glenn whispered, drawing Luce close. "A couple of pretty smart hombres."

"A couple of smart hombres who are going to make a lot of dough," Luce reminded him.

Out on the road once more, and riding toward Cardston, Glenn pondered Luce and his ridiculous perpetual-motion machine. Everyone knew that it was an impossibility. He smiled tenderly—everyone, that is, but Luce.

He guided Buck along the trail.

He'd had to overstay his week a day or so, to cover up for Luce. Money for debts had gone for the perpetual-motion machine. Glenn was around promising payment, seeing that Luce and Abbie would have enough supplies to get along. But he had finally pulled away, explaining carefully to Abbie, as she packed his bedroll with two new blue shirts and half a dozen pairs of wool knitted socks, "I'm riding south across the States' line, Abbie. You see, Sky's been stolen."

He'd had to be careful not to let Luce see his eyes. For in them must have been telltale hints of how badly he needed the money Luce had blown for his machine.

Glenn, smiling ruefully, moved on until he could

sight the town of Cardston in the distance. Doctor Crane would probably be sore because he had overstayed his leave. But there was Doctor Crane coming out of his office to meet him as he rode into the yard, and with the biggest proposition anyone could ever want to have put up to him.

They were back in the doctor's office when he faced Glenn across his desk, his gray eyes carefully surveying the object of his generosity.

"It's a sort of payment for what you did to Peters," Doctor Crane explained, as though it were all settled. "But, it's more than that."

Glenn got the drift at once, and caught his breath.

The doctor was handing him things on a platter: his tuition at Ames, practically a veterinarian's degree for the taking.

"And a partnership when you get out," Doctor Crane's voice came, clipped and final. "Maybe more than that." His eyes crinkled at the corners as they swung meaningly toward the window looking up river toward Daisy De Winton's.

Glenn felt as though he were in a squeeze chute like a yearling steer. He felt foolish, too, foolish as a prairie chicken in a storm.

What would the doctor say when he told him, I— I can't, Doctor. I—I've got to follow the roan?

How could he make him understand that it was Sky who had really brought Peters around. How could he make him see that he couldn't forsake the roan? Quit the horse who had earned him all this. Go on to school and leave the horse once more, to be made a killer in the rodeo circuit?

He opened his mouth to speak.

The doctor waved his hand. "We'll settle the details later, Glenn," he said. He got up.

Glenn rose too, anguish in his heart.

Why was he always in wrong? he wondered.

Doctor Crane turned.

"Wondering why I don't thank him or something," Glenn murmured. Suddenly he took a deep breath, and the words spilled out of him like water running over falls. When he finished, a silence filled the little office.

Even the fox terrier was silent. Rory, who had developed an infection, lay silent in his kennel.

At length, Doctor Crane sat down heavily in his chair. His long fingers picked up a blotter with a dog-food biscuit ad on it, then dropped it.

His lips moved.

"You'll take the buckskin," he said. "And this." He wrote out a check for Glenn's wages and twenty-five dollars extra. "It's the least I can do."

Glenn took the check with taut hands. In his heart, still, lay the thought of keeping friends with Alan. The thought welled to his lips.

"Doctor," he said, "of course I hope I can come back and bring Sky with me. When I do, couldn't we have an understanding? Alan could have full say over the inside work here and I could take the outside, with you the head of it all? It would be only fair to Alan, and we'd both know where we stood all the time."

The doctor raised brightening eyes. His hand stayed Glenn, who would have gone toward the door, not expecting the doctor to give a snap decision.

"You're right, Glenn," he said, after only a moment's thought. "Let me call Alan in right now and get this thing straightened out once and for all."

With Glenn's nod he moved, tall and straight, to the door and called, "Alan! Alan! Come here a minute, will you, please?"

In seconds, Alan, still quiet, still reserved, came through the doorway. His eyes fell questioningly on Glenn and the doctor, then seemed to wait.

"Yes, sir, Doctor," he said.

Doctor Crane spoke quickly, outlining what Glenn had said. When he'd finished, no one spoke for a full minute.

Glenn thought, Have I done it again—pushed Alan still further from me?

Then Alan's soft voice spoke. There was a slight tremor in it that cleared as he went on, "Thank you, Doctor Crane. That's fine."

Two days later, Glenn moved his plodding buckskin down on Browning, a little Montana cowtown lying like a bunch of sprawled dry-goods boxes across the flat prairie. To the south of the town and winding like a huge uncoiled python were the tracks of the Great Northern railway that fed along a hillside to a drab painted depot and beyond, to a bunch of white-washed planked shipping corrals.

Glenn paused a moment, reining in the buckskin, while his moody eyes surveyed the town.

"Browning, then Cutbank," he said hopelessly. "This time I'm trying the railway stations."

Tightening the reins, he rode Buck down to the depot. The agent, an agreeable man who talked like Luce, said, "A blue horse with cropped ears?" He stopped to scratch thinning black hair. "Nope, don't think so."

"Your records?" Glenn persisted. "Look through them."

"Oh, sure, the bills of lading."

Glenn followed him into the depot and sat by the huge potbellied stove while the agent thumbed through a sheaf of waybills.

"Nope," he said to the tune of the chattering telegraph keys. "No horses shipped since that date."

Glenn walked out to Buck. Only the fact that he was doggedly persistent kept him going, that and Law-and-Order's last words before he left: "You keep lookin', Glenn. Sky's a fighter. He'll try for a breakaway. You'll pick up his footmark in some soft ground around a corral."

Snowladen clouds, like smudged sheep, jostled each other across the sky as Glenn climbed to his saddle. "Okay, Cutbank's next," he said, reining the buckskin around.

At Cutbank, Glenn decided to try the corral first, useless as he knew it to be.

Glenn got off Buck at the round shipping corral from which led chutes that fed into the ten stock cars standing on the siding. Glenn walked to the gate.

These cars were Peters,' he knew. Peters would trail his beef across country to Cutbank and ship to Chicago in a stock train powered by a fast, diesel-motored engine.

Glenn hesitated by the gate, his eyes roving for some mark of Sky's hoof. There was no sign, as he knew there would not be. He stepped to the other side of the gate and looked there.

Still no track. Plenty of horse tracks but none of them Sky's.

Glenn turned away to ride down to see the agent. Suddenly he stared at something under the very rim of the plank corral. Just inside the gate, as though the horse had swerved to make a break for freedom, was Sky's hoofmark! A clue!

Glenn could not believe it at first. He walked to it, his eyes staring, then dropped on his knees. The roan had been here. There was the blurred mark of the shoe edge that was thicker than ordinary.

Glenn climbed on Buck and rode down to the depot to face a little man with silver spectacles and sharp blue eyes, who wanted to help at once.

But his help set Glenn back on his boot heels.

"Yes, shipped horses," he said. "Yes, a crop-eared roan who kept trying to break away. Had a big welt along his jaw where he'd been quirt-mauled.

Glenn caught his breath. "By a man with a scar along his cheek?"

"Yes. He was the shipper. Signed himself Jacques Balleau.

Glenn could scarcely squeeze out the word: "Where?" Then he caught the edge of the counter at the agent's disquieting words: "Both ways. He shipped two carloads. One was billed to Palm Springs, the other to Chicago. Here're the car numbers."

Reading the car numbers that seemed to burn into his mind, Glenn got the picture of Sky being beaten into a car by the scar-faced Balleau.

"G.N. 44369, Palm Springs, California," he read. That would be the winter rodeo circuit; Palm Springs, Los Angeles Stock Yards, Salinas. His eyes went on,

"G.N. 22569, Chicago." But why Chicago? Why not New York and Madison Square Garden?

Finally Glenn found his voice.

"Which car did the blue go in?" he asked huskily.

Olson, the agent, hesitated, seeming to search his mind.

Glenn could only wait, his mind tense. So much depended on knowing! If Sky went to California and he went east to look for him, Sky would be in rodeos before he could get to him.

"Dunno," Olson said at length. "Wish I did, boy."

Out in the air again, standing beside Buck, Glenn realized that he'd have to decide for himself which way to go in search of Sky. He'd have to decide fast too, for some place along those rails Sky, in a stock car, was slipping farther and farther from him.

"I'll flip a coin," he said. "Tails I go south, heads east."

Taking a quarter from his pocket, he flipped it into the air. But as it landed in his numb palm, Glenn didn't bother to look at it. For on the air came the bellow of cattle and the wild shouts of punchers herding them toward the shipping corrals. Mingled with the noise was the guttural grunt of the switch engine spotting cars for loading.

Glenn stuffed the coin back in his Levi's and looked up and across the prairie to the herd of approaching cattle, then on to the short burly figure of a man on a big bay horse.

"Peters," Glenn whispered, his heart thudding. "Shipping beef to Chicago."

He moved to mount Buck, and he hardly dared hope that what he thought was true. "Maybe this is a hunch," he breathed, turning Buck toward the herd. "But, it looks like I'm headed east, for Sky."

He rode in a half arc toward the rear of the herd, the big question in his mind: could he land a job with Peters as nursemaid? Would he be on this freight train when it pulled out following the possible trail of the big roan?

17. The Rolling Stock car

PETERS barely nodded as Glenn rode up. He rode stolidly, as though the old resentment against this boy, being indebted to him, still rankled.

Glenn swung his mount and, taking down his lariat end, began, steadily and methodically, to help with the fat steers.

"I have to make the grade," he whispered.

They reached the corrals and the wing out from the gate along which the wild spooky cattle, fresh from the range, crowded toward their doom.

The punchers began pushing them into the corral, a hundred at a time, closing the gate and shoving these hundred cattle into cattle cars, twenty to a car.

It went well, the cattle whooping up the chutes and into the cars with quick wild grace.

Too well, Glenn knew with sinking heart. For Peters had suddenly turned affable. Standing beside a chute, tally stick in hand, he found time to joke with Glenn.

"Hot cakes and coffee off Times Square, eh, Doc?" he called. He'd taken to calling Glenn Doc, ever since the dipping.

Glenn, riding Buck and working in the tiny chute

corral, smiled ruefully; then, with two other punchers on horses, worked doggedly on.

"Yeah," he called back. "Off Times Square." That meant Peters himself was going with the ten loads of cattle. Taking them as far as Chicago and then going on to New York.

Glenn worked on through the afternoon, prodding the cattle up the chutes.

"Going like they're greased," Peters said, leaning over the corral fence to slap Glenn across his shoulders.

"Yeah, like they're greased," Glenn agreed hollowly; then whispered to himself, "And that's the way the train will pull out—without me on the job."

Even the weather turned warm and deceptively mild. "Just the way it is before a storm," Glenn breathed.

At length, as darkness fell, the last steer, with a flourish of his plumed tail, disappeared into the last stock car and the door banged shut.

"Well, Doc"—Peters slapped his thigh with his tally stick and came over to Glenn—"that's over. Now all we've got to do is get'em safe to Chicago."

Glenn felt small and tired. He'd had about enough! The darkness got him, and staring at the swaying stock cars loaded with cattle made him realize that, somewhere, Sky swayed and fought other broncos in a stock car too.

He felt an impulse to swing on Peters and say, "Cut it out. I know you're sore about me saving your skin. But can't you forget it?" He only smiled and nodded his head. "Yeah, that's all we've got to do, Mr. Peters."

Peters grinned and looked off across the darkening

prairie. It was like a brown ocean with tiny swells of hills across which the night wind rippled brown grass. The wind came to Peters. It played along his smooth bronzed face and eyes that suddenly swung on Glenn.

"Well, then"—his voice came with the surprise bark of a pistol shot—"what are we waiting for? Let's get down to the station and sign the stockman's contract. Don't you want to go to Chicago with these cattle, Glenn?"

Hours later, Glenn sat in the stockman's car, listening to the click of the wheels on the rails. Ahead of him rode the two hundred steers in ten stock cars. "Had Sky come this way?" Glenn wondered.

"Feed at Minot and St. Paul," Peters had said, as the long freight train jostled to a start in the darkness. "And good luck finding Sky," he added.

Glenn settled deeper in his seat.

Peters had known about his leaving Doctor Crane. He seemed to know he would be in Cutbank, wanting the job of nursemaid to cattle.

Glenn rolled out his bed on the hard bunk, reciting again the number of Balleau's horse car going east: G.N. 22569. He'd know it any place, even by the light of a switch engine if it ever came to that.

Crawling under the blankets, he lay listening to the monotonous hum of the wheels, wondering if Sky might be at Minot. There was always a chance that a hotbox might have held Balleau up there—freights were always developing delays.

But Minot produced no Sky.

The crews unloaded the steers and fed them.

Glenn walked down to the yards and examined

every stock car in the siding, but none of them read G.N. 22569. Fighting off the feeling that he'd never see Sky again, he came back to help reload the cattle, then climbed into the car used by the stockmen shippers.

The long yellow diesel motor screeched out a whistle, the long train took up slack in the couplings, then slipped quietly on its way.

"St. Paul next stop," Glenn whispered, his throat tight. "Sky will have to be there."

But the layover in St. Paul was a duplicate of that in Minot. The same little restaurant, the same routine of feeding, and the same myriads of stock cars, hundreds here, where in Minot there had been tens, but still not a car numbered G.N. 22569.

Searching to the last minute, walking determinedly up and down along the cars, his eyes checking each one, Glenn's apprehension grew. Sky must have gone to California.

As he climbed the steps of his moving train, a car caught his eyes.

"G.N. 225," his lips read, while his heart leaped to his throat. "Balleau's car. Perhaps Sky's?"

But then Glenn sagged on the steps, for the last two numerals were not 69.

The engine whistle blasted. The train couplings rattled and the train pulled out.

Next stop, Chicago, Glenn thought. Chicago, and Sky must be there! But he knew that he would not be.

Glenn leaped into his car, flung off his clothes, and slipped into his bunk.

Down the aisle by the big stove, now red with fire against the chill outside, three punchers' voices came to Glenn. One was telling in a soft drawl of a wonderful horse he'd owned, his voice betraying, even after all these years, the love for his horse that would not die out.

"Some horse he was," the man's voice carried right into Glenn's bunk. "Big blue with a coat the color of a June sky. And fast, brother. Smart, too. I taught him tricks. Taught him to dance to music, to play dead and lame."

Glenn, catching his breath, rolled to his stomach, pulling the pillow around his head to shut out the puncher's voice. The words seeped through it to him. Glenn rolled to his back.

The puncher went on, "He was stolen from me. I never saw him again. I came east expecting to find him. Like as not he went south."

"Yeah, down to the woolly rodeo circuit in Californy," a second voice chimed in.

"Reckon so," the first puncher's voice came soft and sad, and final. "Like as not they made a roaring outlaw out of him."

Glenn sat up in his bunk, sweat coming out on his forehead. He stared out of the car window at the ghostly telegraph poles slipping past. Suppose Balleau takes Sky to the Madison Square Garden rodeo? Shoves him into the corrals deep beneath the arena there, makes a fighting outlaw of him again? Beats him and holds him for the finals of the bucking-horse contest?

Glenn's nose flattened on the glass, and his lips made dew marks on it as he whispered, "And I'll have to enter the rodeo to win money to buy him, and draw Sky to ride."

Glenn lay back on the bunk, his mind racing over the possibilities, trying to fathom the days ahead.

They reached Chicago the next afternoon and, after what seemed hours of switching, he spotted the cars for unloading to his consigned commission man, Holmes and Company.

Holmes, a big man with a florid face and shock of white hair that reared straight up, met Glenn, taking over the cattle.

Glenn turned the cattle over, impatient to start searching for Balleau's car. Walking down to the ticket office he surrendered his contract, receiving in return a one-way ticket back to Cutbank.

Already it was dark outside.

He moved back to the edge of the platform, his roll and sacked saddle at his feet. Before his eyes and down the track lay the freight depot and, beyond, hundreds of stock cars.

In the distance, a switch engine, busy as a house-wife, bustled along the tracks making up a train of cars.

Glenn walked down the tracks to the freight depot, stowing his saddle and roll beside the drab sooty building.

The habit of days lay upon him.

He turned to the tracks, intending to go in search of Balleau's car, but was stopped by a sign that said, "No trespassing." He sat down on his bedroll, haunted by the thought of Sky in one of those cars, so close and yet so far away.

He gave up hope then, sitting in sodden silence. The switch engine chugged by, snorting. It made more trips, shunting stock cars to the loading track, forming a train that would soon pull out.

With each car, Glenn raise his head, hopefully for a moment, then, reading the numbers, dropped it again in numb despair.

The switching went on.

The darkness grew more intense, lighted only by switch lights dotting the yards in red and green. There was one right in front of Glenn.

Now the bustling switch engine had cars lined up for perhaps a quarter of a mile.

Suddenly a huge black engine came steaming along the main track, sided to the front of the line of box cars, and hitched on with a big bump. It was the engine ready for the run.

The switch engine came running up with a tiny caboose, shunting it to the back end of the train of cars.

"There!" it tooted. "That's the finish. Get going."

The big engine to the front blasted out a whistle. The old familiar taking up of slack in the couplings filled Glenn's ears, and the train began to move, pulling down past him.

He checked the first dozen cars without results. He quit checking then, letting his eyes drop to the worn plank platform, scarred by years of weather and baggage. He'd get a room, Glenn decided, and wait for Peters, who had said, "I'll fly to Chicago, Glenn, and join you. We'll go on and take in the Madison Square Garden rodeo."

The train rolled on, then, as full of whims as any freight, stopped dead. Glenn said impatiently, his heart filled with disappointment, "Beat it. Get going."

He didn't care where. Balleau's car wasn't there, nor Sky.

He raised his eyes in slow moody silence.

Suddenly, he caught his breath, rubbed his eyes and looked again. That car in front of him! The number looked familiar!

"G.N. 22569!" he read. From deep within him a voice prompted, "Sky's car!"

For a moment, Glenn couldn't believe that the car stood there. He would shut his eyes, and when he opened them, it wouldn't be there. Or worse, it would be another car.

He tried it, shutting his eyes, then opening them. The car was still there, Balleau's car.

Glenn gathered himself up and shot across the two tracks separating him from the train. He ran along beside the car, his eyes straining through the night at the slatted sides, his heart beating a tattoo against his ribs.

Horses within snorted. The car rocked from side to side. Glenn, his throat tight, moved close, peering between the slats, calling.

No answer came from within. No nickering response from Sky.

The big engine down the tracks whistled, warning Glenn that the train was pulling out.

He leaned close, calling, "Sky, Sky, are you in there?"

But no Sky answered. It was too dark to see, too dark. And the old familiar sound of the rattling couplings told Glenn that the engine was moving.

He moved along with the car, calling, "Sky, Sky!"

He climbed to the ladder up the side of the car,

putting his head close to the car slats, sticking his hand through.

Suddenly he caught sight of the familiar star in Sky's forehead. A forehead, beaten now, with a big gash along above the eye. Or was it Sky? Other horses had stars.

Glenn put his hand farther through the slats.

The horse sprang back, snorted, then gingerly stretched out his nose, sniffed a moment, then nickered softly, a nicker Glenn would have recognized among a thousand horses.

It was Sky, his Sky. It was his own horse!

For what seemed hours, but must have been but seconds, Glenn clung to the side of the car, while his mind told him he had found a horse he'd never expected to see again.

His heart overflowed with love for the big roan, his roan. He became more precious than Glenn had thought possible. He had to save him now for sure.

The train picked up speed. It was taking Sky out of his life again.

Glenn stared down at the moving ground, his mind racing. His eyes leaped down the long train to the caboose snaking along behind.

"Climb it!" his mind flashed. "Go along with Sky!"

With a bound, Glenn hit the ground, racing for his bedroll and saddle. Grasping them, he ran back to the side of the moving train.

He stood there wondering if he'd get aboard.

The train had picked up speed. Cars whizzed by him with a rushing suck of air. The caboose came at him, tiny, bobbing along like a little red fiend who seemed to dare him to catch its bottom step.

Glenn gathered himself to toss his bedroll to the platform, then suddenly tossed it to the ground. He'd never make it with that. He'd just try to get on with his saddle.

The caboose came on.

Glenn braced himself, then turned to go along with the car, taking it in a swinging stride.

His hand grasped the iron rail, his foot found the bottom step. He had made it! He would go along with Sky! He swung aboard, feeling his body carried along.

But suddenly, as he did so, a man came from inside the caboose, a big man with a scar slash across his cheek. Staring down, not recognizing Glenn at first, he looked more closely by the light of a passing switch light.

"You!" he snarled. Suddenly his foot shot out, caught Glenn full in the chest and sent him sprawling off the train.

Glenn scrambled to his feet, running after the caboose that slipped along just ahead of him.

"I'll buy Sky," he panted, straining for the car end, gaining slightly. "Say anything. Only let me get on."

Reaching the step a second time, he swung aboard.

"Wait! Wait!" Glenn's voice beseeched, his eyes on Balleau. "We can make a deal!"

"You!" Balleau said, and kicked again.

18. Balleau

At TEN minutes to ten that same night, Glenn stepped swiftly along in the La Salle Street depot in Chicago. He paid scant attention to his side, which hurt from the kicks and from his fall off the caboose, or to a cut along his right cheek.

"New York," the placard at the rear of the train said. "Lake Shore Limited."

Glenn walked along the train to a day coach and climbed aboard. Sky was ahead of him on a fast freight. He'd have to hurry to make it to Madison Square Garden by the time the roan did.

Walking down the aisle, Glenn stopped at a seat and tossed his saddle and roll into the rack above him. This done, he sat down heavily, impatient for the train to start.

Peters would come and find him gone, Glenn knew. But he couldn't wait. Balleau had billed Sky's car to the Garden, Glenn had found out from the freight agent. There was no time to lose.

He leaned forward, wondering why the train didn't start. A fat man in the seat opposite him leaned across. He had warm brown eyes and a smile you couldn't ignore.

"It won't start any faster by leaning forward," he said. "Relax cowboy."

Glenn reddened, then leaned back in his seat. He hadn't realized he was so anxious.

"Guess you're right," he agreed, then fell silent.

The train started to move, gliding out of the depot through the maze of tracks, then leveling for the run to New York.

All through the night, with the train lurching, the drummer's breezy voice in his ear at intervals, Glenn rode toward Sky.

The next day passed as in a vacuum. Then shortly before six o'clock that evening, the crack train glided into the tunnel leading to Grand Central Station at Forty-second and Lexington.

"Soon be in," the fat drummer said. "Yep, soon be into the greatest little old city in the world."

Glenn nodded, hearing the dull roar of the electric train drawing them in. Would Sky have arrived? How would he take to the truck bringing him down from Mott Haven?

"Yeah, soon be in," he replied.

To fill in time and quiet the tumult within him, Glenn rose to walk down the aisle to the washroom. Drinking deeply of ice water, he washed his face, combed his thick red hair, and smoothed down the new blue windbreaker Abbie had made him.

The train was slowing down as he came back to his seat.

The fat man said, "You ridin' for the Garden and the rodeo, cowboy?"

Glenn paid attention only to the fact that the train came to a halt. Was he riding in the rodeo? He hoped not. Not if he could make some kind of deal with Balleau for Sky. What he wanted was to high-tail it back to Cardston and Crane and get on with his life's work.

"I—I'm headed for Madison Square Garden," he answered truthfully.

"Well, good luck," the fat man said. "And by this picture of an outlaw you'll need it. He's called the Phantom Roan. Want to see?"

Glenn avoided looking at the extended paper. All he wanted was to get to Sky, fast. But he didn't want to be rude, either.

He hesitated.

"I get it"—the fat man pocketed the paper. "You want to keep your nerve?"

Glenn gave him a wintry smile as the image of Balleau's sneering face came before his eyes.

"Yeah, that's it," he whispered, reaching for his bedroll and saddle. "That's what I have to do, keep my nerve." He had only about forty dollars left to offer Balleau for Sky.

"Well, so long. See you in the saddle," the drummer said and was gone down the aisle.

"Yeah, in the saddle," Glenn agreed. "At Cardston on Sky; on duty," he added to himself.

Grabbing his bedroll and saddle he joined the file of people making their way from the daycoach, up the ramp, and finally out to the taxi stand.

The weight of the city seemed to crush Glenn. For a fleeting moment he felt that he was licked. Balleau wouldn't do a thing. Sky would go on into the rodeo and come out a fighting, raving, maniac horse, ruined for all time.

People jostled Glenn, turning in annoyance, then smiled at the tall sturdy puncher before them.

"Sorry, cowboy," they said, and hurried on.

Glenn shrugged off his depression and moved out to the cab stand. He couldn't afford it, but he was in a hurry.

Tall buildings in the night seemed to weight him down. Off to the north the twin towers of the Waldorf Hotel loomed.

A Sky Top cab came up.

Glenn climbed in.

"Madison Square Garden, cowboy?" the cab driver asked easily.

Glenn nodded, feeling the shake of his neck as the car zoomed out into Park Avenue, then threaded its way toward Broadway. A dogged hope rose in him.

Through the glass in the roof, Glenn's eyes might have seen the tall spire of the Empire State Building.

Glenn sat in the crawling cab, blind to the beauty of the city and the bedlam around him. His mind seethed with plans.

Would Sky be here? And Balleau, what would he say to him? Surely there was some right thing to say to win.

The cab had crossed Fifth Avenue, moving west. "This is Times Square," the cabby flung back at Glenn. "Broadway and Forty-second Street. Say you want to meet a guy; you stand on this corner long enough and he'll come by."

Glenn's eyes took in the Times Tower Building, swung along Broadway with its lighted theatre marquees; a billboard with RODEO in big red letters and a picture of a horse met his eyes.

Glenn hastily looked away.

"Yeah?" he politely replied to the cabman. "That so?"

The cab turned north on Broadway.

"I was at the Rodeo last night," the driver said. "The way they treat those bucking horses, crowdin' 'em into chutes, buccaroos all over the place, yellin' at them! No wonder they're outlaws."

Glenn felt a tug at his heart.

"I like Gene Autry myself, or Roy Rogers. I got a big bang out of his horse Trigger doin' tricks, dancin' to music. Why don't they have more of that?"

Deep within Glenn, the idea lodged.

"Yeah, why don't they?" he demanded.

The cab rolled off Broadway at Fifty-ninth Street and pulled to the curb.

For the swift second it took the cabman to reach for the catch releasing the door, Glenn sat staring at the entrance to Madison Square Garden.

How different from last year. Then, with the Triangle riders, it had all been a lark. Just a boy from the Alberta range trying to have some fun and see New York. Back then it hadn't mattered that the outlaw horse fought him. It had been what he'd wanted.

Now, the thought that the horses fought, that Sky might have to get into the arena and fight, made Glenn feel queer inside.

"Funny," he whispered. "Guess I've grown up."

"Okay, cowboy," the driver's voice roused Glenn. "I'll be lookin' for you on an outlaw."

Again Glenn felt that queerness seize him.

"Sky?" he wondered.

Paying the driver, he was conscious of people already drifting into the lobby for tonight's rodeo show. Again Glenn was conscious of a horse's picture on a billboard in the lobby. The words, Fighter, Alberta Outlaw came to him, the name Phantom Roan. He turned away from them, feeling slightly sick.

"Balleau," he whispered, "I've got to see him quick."

Picking up his bedroll and saddle, he made his way into the Garden and on down to the corrals one floor below the street level.

Two riders on horseback hazed a bunch of wild mustangs, bays and sorrels with a sprinkling of blacks, up the ramp for the chutes and the evening's entertainment.

Glenn caught his breath, staring at the wild horses. Was Sky there?

He moved on down the ramp to the corrals, his eyes searching, his mind filled with what he was going to say to Balleau.

Then suddenly a truck came rumbling in, and another, and another. Sky must be in one of them, Glenn sensed at once.

Piling his saddle and roll along a fence, he moved toward the trucks. He would help unload, maybe get in a word to Sky to soothe him.

But as the first truck rolled to a stop, Balleau boiled from the seat and, hitting the cement floor, planted himself solidly in front of Glenn.

In the electric light, his scarred face wore an assured smile. Nobody knew Glenn around here. Balleau was in. But Balleau wanted to play with him. Things were going well with him. He could have a little fun.

"What you want, kid?" he asked.

Glenn eyed Balleau, trying to figure him out. He opened his mouth to say, "I want my horse back. He would have died there in the river bottom but for me."

Balleau beat him to it.

"Sure," he said. "You saved my horse's life. For that," he leered at Glenn, "I will let you ride him in the rodeo."

His laugh carried above the roar of Sky's hoofs coming down the ramp with other horses and into the corrals.

Glenn leaned against the fence, weak with desire for his roan, and with but one thought filling his mind: how to keep from doing just what Balleau was going to force him to do.

"You owe me something for saving him," he demanded of Balleau. His eyes followed Sky who turned his head for a brief instant, nickering at him, before he sprang away to dodge the kick of another horse.

Balleau's heavy face scowled.

"I owe you nothing," he said. "He was my horse. That C brand is mine. He is still my horse."

Glenn knew he wasn't getting any place. He pulled out his slim roll of forty dollars: three tens, a five, some ones and a little "chicken-feed."

"Here," he said. "Anything more you want beyond this forty, I'll earn. You can garnishee my wages with Doctor Crane."

Balleau's scorn was something to see.

"For the job you don't have?" he said. "And this forty for the horse, the worst tiger of the whole bunch of outlaws?"

"I'll work, I'll slave. You can follow me and collect," Glenn pleaded.

Balleau's shrug told him he was through.

Glenn, his hope gone, stared out past Balleau and, through the light haze, caught sight of Sky once more. The roan had lost his shine. His coat was dull and his eyes in the light had a greenish hating glow.

He was really then, the Phantom Roan. Just a horse who had come into his life as a shadow along the river and would go out the same way here in the uncertain light of this basement.

Glenn said hoarsely, "How much, if I had the money?"

Balleau's eyes narrowed, his thick lips moving. "A thousand dollars," he said. "Cash."

Glenn caught his breath. Some way, somehow, he must get it. Maybe Luce had made his money on one of his machines?

He'd wire him.

"It's a deal," he said to Balleau. "Shake!"

Balleau parried Glenn's hand, and his words dropped like rocks on the boy's consciousness. "But only after the rodeo, kid."

Glenn, his heart in his mouth, stared as Balleau shuffled in his pockets, then brought out a program.

"You see, kid," he went on. "The roan is billed for Saturday night. He's the outlaw from Alberta, the Phantom Roan. He'll go on as scheduled. It's in my contract."

Out on the street again, Glenn hailed a second cab, blurting out the name of the café Peters had mentioned to him and which came to his mind now.

Stowing the stuff in the cab, he climbed in and sat

in dull misery as the cab crawled through the evening crowd along Eighth Avenue.

He was in it now for sure, Glenn knew.

The roan would be ridden Saturday night, and by whom? Well, there was silent Joe Bailey of the Panhandle. Glenn's eyes caught his familiar name on the program. Larry Parks from Alberta would ride, and, of course, Balleau.

"And yourself," a voice within Glenn prompted. "If you want to get money to buy Sky."

It seemed then, as the cab stopped in front of a blue and red neon sign blinking out READY ROOM, that a giant noose had been flung around Glenn pulling him toward the Madison Square Garden arena and Sky.

"That will be seventy-five cents," the taxi man said. "And good luck in your ride Saturday night."

He laughed as Glenn's eyes met his.

"I saw you ride last year, kid," he said. "Alberta Kid. They've got you billed for Saturday and on some horse."

Again he looked at the program.

"Sky," Glenn whispered, "and me. How did they know I'd be riding?"

"Dunno, kid, but good luck. By the looks of that outlaw, the Phantom Roan, you'll need it."

Glenn, picking up his saddle and roll, moved across the sidewalk and to the READY ROOM counter that made a U curve around a center broiler of gleaming copper and a huge open barbecue.

"Hello, Champ," a familiar voice said.

Glenn's head shot up from stowing his stuff around him.

"Millie Stiles," he said, his eyes going over the girl in a white frilled apron, whose hands already spread out silver and a glass of water with speed and quiet.

"How'd I get here?" Millie laughed. "On the train. It runs from Macleod, you know." Her voice took on a serious note. "I'm working to save money for a course as a laboratory technician."

Glenn could only stare at her, little Millie Stiles of Macleod. He used to help her with her physiology experiments.

"I'm—I'm glad to see you, Millie," Glenn said.

"I am glad to see you, too," Millie said, softly. "Though I knew you were coming. Mr. Peters wired me. Said to feed you well, that you were going to win the bucking-horse title at Madison Square Garden."

Glenn stared at her, picking up the menu and, without looking at it, ordered thick steak and French fries, a glass of milk and apple pie á la mode.

So that explained the program, with his name entered as a contestant.

"Oh, he did," Glenn breathed.

Millie nodded her small head crowned by an immense braid of shining brown hair.

"And you are, of course." She went for his order, and came back with it.

People around stared at Glenn.

One man came over, fishing out a program. "You the Alberta Kid?" He was good-natured, friendly. "And is this horse as wild as the program says?"

Glenn opened his mouth.

"What do you mean, wild?" his lips wanted to say. "He's swell. He's the gentlest horse in the world, inside."

He stared at the man's laughter, and the laughter that went around the room. He suddenly realized that he must have said it out loud.

"I know, inside." The man grinned. "But how about the outside, just under that blue hide of his?"

"That's mean," a voice said from the doorway, and into the café came Balleau, striding right up to Glenn. "Mean," he repeated with a sneer. "And do you ride him Saturday night or do I?"

Glenn sat quietly, while his mind raced over plans. Balleau would beat Sky, making him frantic as the two days went by before Saturday night.

If there were some way to prevent this? Suddenly he turned in his swivel stool, his eyes on Balleau's.

"You lay off Sky," he bargained, "and I'll ride him."

Balleau's eyes held to Glenn's for seconds, then slid away as he moved to the counter well down from Glenn.

"Maybe I will, then again, maybe I won't," he said.

19. Rodeo

Two DAYS later Glenn, with Millie beside him, walked slowly into the foyer of the Madison Square Garden arena. These last few days, it seemed to him, had gone by with the speed of gaunt wolves leaping across a forest clearing.

After leaving the café that night, he had gotten a room with Millie's mother, who ran a rooming house.

The next day, he'd gone out with Millie to the top of the Empire State Building. At her insistence, and because Luce would be hurt later on if he hadn't, Glenn had wired him for money.

But overlooking the city, Glenn's eyes swung toward Eighth Avenue and Madison Square Garden where Sky was corralled, helpless before Balleau's cruelty. And the words of his wire: DEAR LUCE, I NEED A THOUSAND DOLLARS QUICK. HOW ABOUT THE MACHINE? had sounded foolish and hopeless.

Now, Glenn took Millie's slender arm and guided her along the foyer through the afternoon crowd.

People turned to watch this tall muscular red-head in windbreaker, high-heeled boots, and Levi's, and the little girl in a red dress, with masses of light-brown hair under a big black hat.

"Sorry, cowboy," a man apologized, jostling Glenn.

"Hey, that's the Alberta Kid!" a freckle-faced boy of twelve shouted. "Hey, can I have your autograph?" His pink program was thrust at Glenn's troubled face.

Glenn took the program and signed it with the stubby pencil, telling himself that something had to happen, some miracle before tonight, to save Sky and not betray the roan's trust in him.

But time was closing in on him with the speed of a winter nightfall. It was the last call before disaster.

The boy's voice penetrated Glenn's mind with the sharpness of a skinning knife blade. "You gonna ride the roan outlaw tonight, that tiger horse?"

Glenn stared down at the boy, and his heart inside him seemed to turn over. His dogged hope of something happening to save Sky lessened.

"Ride Sky?" he whispered to himself. "Fight him in the arena. Make boys like this one think he is really an outlaw instead of a swell pal, a wonder horse that could do tricks."

"I—I don't know," he managed, thrusting the program at the boy. "I—don't know."

He fled up the ramp with Millie to their seats in the great oval-shaped arena. As he helped Millie with her coat, and slumped into his seat, the smell of tanbark came up to him. He'd had an idea for two days that he'd get a break. He had held onto it. But now he wondered. His eyes moved to the chutes at each end of the arena, now empty. In the dim light, he tried to think, to plan, but nothing came of it.

Cameron's Cowboy Band had just come in. After a moment's tuning up they began to play the *Blue Danube*.

Glenn caught his breath. It was Sky's piece. What a kick he would get out of dancing to it here.

The lights dimmed still further and, under the giant arcs that flooded the arena, the grand entry began. Contestants, and exhibition riders filed in, a moving, beautiful flow of horses and their riders in a giant serpentine.

Glenn stared at it and wondered where Sky was.

The voice of Abe Wright, the announcer, came on the microphone, from the stand just over the north chutes. His words drifted out to Glenn, sitting just a few rows back of the band. They meant nothing now but the rush of time moving relentlessly on toward this evening Abe introduced the judges: "Ladies and Gentlemen, Carl Walsh from New Mexico, Joe Dorsey of Arizona, Peter Lawrence of Montana." He finished amidst a splatter of applause.

The arena cleared The first event, the Cowboy's Bareback Riding, began.

Millie whispered, "Luce must have your wire by now, and sent you an answer."

Glenn nodded dully. There'd be no wire. Mrs. Stiles at the rooming house would wait in vain for anything to send on to him here. He tried to fix his mind on the rodeo.

Riders came out of the chutes, balanced on their roaring, bellowing, bucking mounts. Sometimes they "stayed" the full ten seconds until the blast of the horn. Again, in a series of moves much like those of jointless rag dolls, they tumbled from their mounts.

A man three seats behind Glenn boomed out, as a slim rider rode the "distance," "Ride 'em cowboy."

A second man beside him with a sharp voice chimed in, "Nice goin', puncher!"

They seemed to know good riding when they saw it.

Glenn could not join in. They would see Sky tonight, he allowed with a sick feeling through him. What would they think of letting a pal be turned into an outlaw—after he had promised Sky he would never hit the chutes again!

For nothing would happen to keep him from riding Sky, he was convinced of that.

The horse quadrille came and passed, then Gene Autry with his trick sorrel, Champion. Glenn became more than ever convinced of doom.

He could scarcely watch the smart dark-colored sorrel with the white stockings go through his tricks: sitting on a chair, playing lame, dropping on the tanbark to simulate an Indian fight, then dancing to music.

A lump came into Glenn's throat, as he watched. Girls and boys around him went wild with applause.

"Sky," Glenn whispered, "Sky, you're as gentle and wonderful as Champion, if they only knew it."

The calf roping began.

Glenn, his mind still searching for a way out, watched the swift flight of Des Harmon's body on his wild palomino, Rocket. The mad run of the Brahma calf. Then the catch and tie in twenty-two seconds flat. Caught the swift pat of affection and the rubbing muzzle of Rocket afterward, as Des, down from Alberta, defended his title won at Lethbridge.

"Sky's that kind of horse too, but no one will know it," Glenn whispered, his eyes following the light grace of the sinister El Gato making his first tie in Des' time.

Too soon the calf roping was over.

Acrobatic trick riders came flashing into the arena. Dressed in white buckskin, mounted on milk-white horses, the one man and two girls made a stunning entry.

Tiny Ross on his pinto Shetland followed and got a big hand.

Glenn slowly surveyed them, as the courage that had bolstered him faded away like trailing cattle over a hill.

The two girls rode, doing tricks. The man caught them with his lariat as they dashed past. Tiny Ross, on his Shetland, rode past, upside down, balanced on his galloping mount.

The audience applauded madly. Glenn clapped mechanically, for slowly, surely, time was closing in.

Then suddenly, into the silence following the exit of the acrobats, Abe Wright's voice dropped in the final event of the afternoon:

"Ladies and Gentlemen," his voice said, "the Cowboy's Saddle Bronco Riding Contest."

Glenn's somber eyes swung to the chutes, straining under the mad rattle of riders saddling up.

A rider in chute one was dropping his worn saddle on a horse's back.

The bronco in the chute lunged, bellowed, and fought. Glenn caught sight of its ears laying flat as it reared high in the chute. He clutched his seat with tense hands.

"Tonight, those ears will be Sky's," he whispered to

himself. "And what will happen when his eyes see that it's me!"

A groan escaped him. It was no use. He was through. He was trapped. No help was coming.

He covered his groan with a cough, grabbing a red bandanna Abbie had hemmed for him.

"Tanbark dust," he explained to Millie. "Got in my throat."

She nodded, but refused to turn toward him her telltale eyes.

"Olson, from Alberta, from chute one," came Abe's voice. "On Eggbeater!"

Olson gave a good ride under generous applause.

"Silent Joe Bailey, on You First. You first over his ears." Abe announced.

Bailey gave a good ride to the titter of amusement, then the sober silence that followed. He went the "distance," a short powerful man with a beautiful rhythm in the saddle to the fighting bronco.

"A good ride!" the heavy-voiced man behind Glenn boomed. It sought Glenn out and riveted his attention.

It didn't warn him of what was to follow.

The sharp-voiced man said, "You ain't seen nothin' yet."

"No?"

The man's next words jerked Glenn up in his seat as though he'd just tied his rope on a thousand-pound steer.

"No. Wait till the Alberta Kid rides that Alberta Outlaw, that Phantom Roan, tonight."

Glenn gulped. but more was to follow. Words that poured over him as scalding lead might have.

"But I ain't goin' to see it," the heavy voice boomed. "I was in Alberta inspecting a band of sheep—heard about a boy studying to be a vet and the horse he'd cured. He was a beautiful horse, powerful but gentle. I saw him. And listen to this! He was a roan! And now he turns up here, an outlaw—I saw that Balleau quirting him—and the boy shows up to ride him. Looks to me like a dirty deal between Balleau and the Alberta Kid, especially if the horse remembers him and won't fight. It's going to look great to the gallery, but like rotten business to me. Selling out his friend! Betraying a horse that trusted him."

"Well, I should say! If the Kid has any decency at all, he'll never let his horse hit the chute. The roan would come out of it a raring, tearing killer," the sharp-voiced man answered. "Goin' to be a vet." Scorn filled his voice. "Fine vet he'll make. I always thought veterinarians loved horses and hated to see them made outlaws."

"Where'd you get this story?" boomed the first voice.

Glenn held his breath, though he knew the answer before the man spoke.

"Right from Balleau, that's where. What guys will do for money these days!"

Outside, minutes later, walking along with people leaving the garden, Millie by his side, Glenn knew what he had to do.

At Eighth Avenue, he turned to Millie.

"Wait here a minute, please. I'll be right back."

"It took him but a few minutes to reach the business offices of Madison Square Garden and a door marked, MANAGER.

Voices came through the door.

Glenn paused a moment then, taking a deep breath, opened the door and walked in.

Ted Weadick, a hat tipped back on his head, looked up at Glenn through deep blue eyes. He had the look of a prairie man even here on his job. Sunburned skin stretched lean along his jaw.

Across the room, Balleau swung to face Glenn.

Glenn stared, then flushed. For a moment, he considered, then thrusting back his shoulders said, "I can't ride the roan, Mr. Weadick. I'm sorry." Then he added, "The roan shouldn't be ridden at all. He's too good a horse for that."

Weadick half rose from his chair in surprise. A dull red crawled up his neck. His eyes darkened obstinately.

"But you're billed," he protested. "The audience! How will we explain?"

"Tell 'em the truth," Glenn said. "That the roan's wonderful, too wonderful to go back to being an outlaw."

Weadick shook his head stubbornly.

"Oh, no," he said. "We can't do that. Skip it, Barnes." Outlaws were moneymakers.

"But," Glenn persisted.

Weadick leaned across the desk.

"No!" he snapped. "And you won't ride him, eh?" Glenn shook his head.

"Okay," Weadick sank back to his seat, tipping his hat farther on his head. "That's settled. But somebody will."

"Sure, somebody will," Balleau stepped forward. "I will." His cruel lips broke into a hateful smile.

Glenn looked from Weadick to Balleau, then back to Weadick. He'd made an awful mistake. He'd made things a lot worse for Sky.

"I've changed my mind," he said slowly. "I will ride him, after all."

Weadick shook his head.

"Oh, no," he said. "No, you won't. Balleau'll ride him."

Balleau would drive the horse crazy, and it would look like a good fight.

20. Shoot the Brute

GLENN never knew what happened between the time he left Weadick's office and when he sat petrified in the seat that night at Madison Square Garden. No telegram had come from Luce. It seemed to him, sitting there with Millie in her red dress, that the rodeo had been going on for a thousand years.

Roping calves and acrobatic stunt horses raced before his eyes. The sound of Abe Wright's voice and the thunderous applause after each event drummed in his ears.

Glenn sat in dull anguish, remembering Balleau's sneering, "I'll ride the roan, Weadick."

His eyes never left the runway up which Sky would be forced into the bucking chutes.

Suddenly Balleau swaggered up the runway and to the corrals. Glenn, in his seat close to the north chutes, very close to Abe Wright's announcing stand, caught the glint of Balleau's spurs against the arc lights.

Before he could more than catch his breath, the announcer said, "Ladies and Gentlemen, the next event will be," his voice hushed for dramatic effect, then filled in, "the Bronco Riding Contest with saddles. And a special announcement: The Alberta Kid isn't riding the roan. He isn't riding at all!"

Glenn felt that if the crowd only knew about Sky they wouldn't want him to ride him. That murmur of disappointment sweeping across the audience like wind across tall grass would change to cheers.

"But wait?" Abe Wright's voice came again, filled with assurance for the crowd. "The roan will be ridden, and by Balleau."

A fine dew formed just under the edge of Glenn's thick red hair. He'd gotten Sky into this.

Balleau, spurs jingling, moved across to the chutes. A burly man, a cruel man, who would make Sky an outlaw for as long as he lived.

Glenn sat numbed and silent.

Suddenly shouts came, the whoop of cowboys, then the rush of horses into the chutes. Was the roan there?

His pulse racing, Glenn looked in vain for that big blue body. Maybe, he thought, with a grain of comfort, Sky had twisted a leg?

But suddenly he slumped in his seat. For the big roan came sweeping up the runway and into the corral. Even at that distance, Glenn could feel the surge, see the power under those silken muscles.

Glenn gave up hope then. Sky would fight. Balleau would ride him and there wasn't any way to stop it. Luce wasn't going to answer. There wouldn't be any wire relayed to the Madison Square box office, and out to Abe Wright.

The big roan leaped against the squeeze chute. He fought. He reared.

"Sky! Sky!" Glenn whispered in stricken horror.

Millie, beside him, sat clutching his arm. He had finally told her all about himself and Sky that afternoon.

Balleau climbed over the chute, saddle in hand.

Now they had put a hackamore on Sky, one with a regulation one-inch braided-grass rope.

Sky fought it, but Balleau forced it over his cropped ears. Now the saddle, a single-rig, scarred, raw-leather round-skirted, buckaroo model, settled on his arched back.

Abe's voice came again.

"Out of chute one: Bailey on Battlewagon."

Glenn had eyes only for Sky. He could only see Balleau slowly, silently, implacable as the tracking cougar, go down inside the chute and force his saddle on the fighting roan, cinching it tight.

Seconds seemed hours to Glenn.

Sky would fight Balleau to the last ditch, he knew. He might throw him, then wheel to trample him into the tanbark. And people wouldn't understand that it was just the big roan fighting back as he'd been trained to do.

A horn rasped.

Bailey had "lasted" his ride.

Balleau, Glenn sensed, would "last" too. Why had he failed Sky? He should have gone on to ride the big roan himself, not gone to Weadick. He should have done anything but let this big burly man, with evilness in his heart and cruelty in his mind, ride him.

Sky was saddled.

Balleau, rope in hand, sat astride him.

A hush settled over the haze-drenched arena.

Abe's voice, almost whispering, tense, intent, breathed, "Out of chute two, Balleau on"—Abe's voice rose sharply—"on Phantom Roan!"

For seconds, it seemed to Glenn, the gate would not open. A fierce joy filled him.

Balleau had lost his nerve. He was afraid. He was crawling off!

Relief gushed through Glenn like the first spring freshet down Milk River's gravel bed.

Sky was saved! And there was a uniformed usher going toward Abe with a yellow sheet of paper in his hand.

The telegram from Luce flashed through Glenn's mind. It had been sent on from the boarding house.

But suddenly, Balleau climbed back into his saddle. Glenn slumped to his seat.

Balleau had just adjusted his stirrup. He was settling deeply into his saddle.

And the usher had given the paper to Abe who smiled, thrusting it into his pocket. It was nothing.

Glenn's groan was drowned in the creak of the gate's opening. Sky's gate it was, with Balleau in the saddle.

A hush, like that of the silence between two mountains, settled over the audience. Glenn gripped his seat. Then somehow sensing something was going to happen, he got up and ran automatically toward the arena. It was as though he knew Sky would need him.

Suddenly the great horse gathered himself. His huge, heavy muscled body trembled, his head dropped. He seemed to explode in terrible violence.

He came out of the chute with a mighty bound. High into the arc-lighted air he leaped. Higher and higher his body soared, a great blue column of protest in the searing light, then suddenly he came down.

No man could withstand that jar, Glenn knew as he

raced for the arena. He hit the tanbark and ran across it to Sky. Balleau's body snapped. His head fell backward. He slumped in the worn saddle and washed from the seat to the tanbark. A little puff of dust arose where he fell.

A gasp riffled over the crowd like wind across treetops.

It turned to horror as Sky, quick as a flash, turned to trample Balleau.

"He'll kill him!" came the cry.

But Glenn had reached Sky. Heedless of his own danger, he thrust his body between Sky and Balleau.

"No, Sky!" he cried. "No!"

It was only a second. It was only enough to allow Balleau's escape as hands dragged him free.

Pickup riders forced their horses between the roan and the man whom he knew only as an enemy. One who had quirted him without mercy, beaten him, tormented him.

Ropes slipped over his fighting head; lariats licked at his feet, ensnaring them.

The roan still fought on.

"Outlaw! Outlaw!" yelled the crowd.

The three judges rode up. One of them, receiving a nod from his fellows, snapped, "Shoot the brute. Drag him down the runway and shoot him!"

Glenn stood stunned.

But Sky wasn't an outlaw. He was good, just fighting as he'd been trained to do from early colthood. A sob shook Glenn. He found himself shouting, "No, don't shoot him! He's good! He's wonderful!"

His voice was drowned under the noise of the crowd and the shouts of the cowboys dragging Sky from the arena. Surrounded with ropes, pulled, pushed, tugged at. Sky was being slowly forced from the chutes and down the runway.

Following him. limping, but on his feet and his face contorted with vengeful rage, walked Balleau.

With a lunge, Glenn ran down the runway. Oblivious to Sky's berserk rage and its danger to him, he moved swiftly after the throng.

Would he be too late? Would Balleau already have wreaked his revenge?

Glenn ran till he came up with the knot of people. They had Sky down now, wrapped in ropes.

Balleau moved toward the prostrate roan, a gun in his hands.

Glenn threw himself at the men encircling Sky.

"Let me through!" he panted. "Let me through!"

The line held.

"Stay out of this, kid," a man ordered, thrusting Glenn back. "He'll kill you, too, this mad roan."

Glenn, thinking only of Sky, wrenched free.

He wormed his way through the men to the roan. He knelt beside the sweating, struggling horse. He put his arm around the lathered neck.

For an instant, the roan stopped fighting. A muffled nicker of recognition came from his foaming lips.

Something welled within Glenn then. In the sweat, the dust and noise. they were back on the prairie, Sky and he, down by the river with the roan's soft muzzle caressing his cheek. The smell of woodsmoke was in the air.

Glenn leaped to his feet, his eyes blazing, his hands pushing people back, his body blocking Balleau. He turned and began untying Sky.

"Come on, men," he ordered. "Get these ropes off this horse. I'll show you what he is."

Hands leaped to free the roan. Sky struggled, trembling to his feet.

"Come on, Sky," Glenn breathed, slapping the roan's steaming neck. "Do this for me, Sky."

He was in the saddle.

He paused, wondering what to do.

Suddenly from the runway came the answer.

"The band," Glenn whispered. "Sky, it's music. Come on." His words spilled into the roan's cropped ears.

The horse swung and together they swept up the runway toward the sound of distant music.

A gate barred their way.

"Up, boy," Glenn called, pulling the rope sharply. The roan soared over it, into the arena and around its oval; running beautifully, a phantom horse under the arcs.

A gasp filled the domed arena. The crowd watched fascinated as boy and horse swept again around the oval.

They found their voices, shouting, "The outlaw! The Phantom Roan, the terrible outlaw!"

"Ladies and Gentlemen—" Abe's voice began, then sputtered, the microphone a dead thing before him.

A cheer broke out.

The man's rasping voice came clear, "Wonder horse!"

It caught Glenn's ears. He leaned over, "Let's show 'em, Sky."

With swelling heart, he moved the roan to the center of the arena as he had seen Gene Autry do with

Champion. He made Sky lie down, pretending they were Indian fighting. He led him, the big horse pretending lameness.

Then suddenly the band struck up the *Blue Danube*.

Glenn caught a flash of a red dress and knew that Millie must have gone down to Cameron to ask for it. He waved his hat.

The roan moved around the arena to the music, head erect, tail switching, in a beautiful dance step.

Boys and girls cheered. They whistled.

Abe's voice came again.

"I'm told his name is Sky," his voice said. "The boy saved his life when the horse was ill and hurt. Balleau, who had left him to die, stole him back. Let's give boy and horse a great big hand."

Glenn stopped Sky. He pulled the rope, and the big horse reared, walking on his hind legs before the stands.

Thunderous applause followed. But suddenly the noise died out and Glenn, swinging Sky toward the gate, felt that same dull misery grip him. The roan was still Balleau's. He'd have to ride Sky down the runway and turn him over to Balleau.

He moved along the side of the arena, all the life and pleasure in the roan's performance gone from him.

He reached the gate over which Sky had soared so short a time before. But there was Abe's voice once more, stopping him with, "Just a moment, Glenn. Hold it."

A man leaned close, talking to Abe.

The next few moments were a blur to Glenn. He never would know how it happened.

There was a flash of a red dress going across the arena to Abe. It was Millie, of course, and she was talking to the judges. An usher came from the office to the stand, and even Balleau sidled in.

Abe's voice came again, "Ladies and Gentlemen." His voice rose with pleasure. "A special award to the Alberta Kid: five hundred dollars."

Listening to Abe's voice, Glenn figured swiftly. It was wonderful, but just half enough to satisfy Balleau.

"Five hundred for the Alberta Kid and his horse! No, wait, not his horse, but Balleau's horse. But I'm sure Balleau will sell him. How about it, Balleau?" Abe turned to Balleau, shaming him, putting the heat on.

The man reddened, but shook his head stubbornly. "He's worth a thousand dollars," he growled.

"A thousand dollars," Glenn whispered.

They weren't anywhere near a deal.

"Wait," Abe's voice again came clear. "Here's a wire for Glenn Barnes, the Alberta Kid." He extended it to Glenn. "Read it aloud, Alberta. Tell us the news."

Glenn prodded Sky to the edge of the stand, his heart thudding under his windbreaker. The slip of paper Abe had put so casually into his pocket? And he was grinning now!

Tearing it open, the black typed words on the yellow sheet seemed to leap at his eyes.

"We're in, partner, struck it rich," Glenn read, and caught the saddle horn with his other hand. Who would have thought it, the little red and white perpetual-motion machine coming through!

But it had. Triumph surged in him.

He raised his head to Abe, his eyes going on to Balleau.

"Five hundred, no, four hundred. I've got to have freight money. Four hundred cash, Balleau," he said. "Six hundred balance in three weeks time."

In the silence from the microphone the crowd hushed.

Balleau looked around.

Men's eyes ringed him. He wanted to say, "All cash or no deal," but the crowd frightened him into it. He nodded his head and said, grudgingly, "Okay, Barnes, it's a deal, but you'd better have that six hundred."

Ten days later, Glenn, on Sky, rode up the trail and reined the big roan into the *Shoestring* yard.

A light wind blew down from the snowbanked Rockies. The hills back of the river lay brown and beautiful, dotted with white-faced cows free of blemish.

Glenn reined Sky through the little barbed-wire gate, an urgency filling him. He had stopped off at Cardston, where the doctor had been glad to see him.

He had wanted to stay, with the doctor's talking of plans for the future that included him; with Barbara bursting in, exclaiming over Sky and what had happened to him at Madison Square Garden.

"The papers were full of it," she teased. "You're a celebrity."

Alan, too, chimed in, friendly, really friendly at last. "It's nice to have you back, big shot."

Glenn moved Sky down toward the little ranch house. They were all coming out for a feast later in the day. Alan was bringing his accordion. Law-and-

Order would come too, and Rory, the big Chesapeake, soon to go home well.

Glenn checked Sky at the battered pine door. It wouldn't be long, now. That little old machine would give him the "word." He could scarcely believe it.

Luce opened the door and stood there, blinking like a big bear.

"Glenn?" he said in surprise. Then seeming to recover, he added, "Come down to the barn. I've got something to show you." Excitement surged in his voice.

It spilled over into Glenn, who waved to Abbie and said, "Just a minute." Then he followed Luce's burly frame to the door of the little log barn.

"Okay," he said, dismounting, his throat tight, and his mind filled with that little red-and-white machine. Balleau had to be paid six hundred cold dollars. "Okay, bring on the wonder gadget."

Luce's eyes clouded, puzzled, for a moment, then cleared. "There's no gadget, Glenn. It's this." He waved a hand to the left.

Glenn's eyes swung to a patch of dried-up Canada thistle.

"It was the stuff in the green can that killed 'em. The hardest weed in all Canada to kill," Luce said. "We're offered ten thousand dollars for the formula and an interest in the company."

Glenn's first impulse was to say, "Just for tossing an old can into a patch of weeds, you get this, Luce." The words died on his lips.

Surely it was an accident that Luce had done it and struck it rich. But other men had struck pay dirt in just such freaky ways.

Glenn wanted to say, "Luce, you're a smart man." That, too, died unsaid. Luce wasn't a smart man.

Suddenly Abbie's erect figure in the doorway caught his eyes. Abbie who had always believed in Luce.

"Okay, Luce," Glenn said softly. "We'll take it, eh?"

"Which makes us a couple of pretty smart hombres, partner?" Luce asked. Glenn's answer seemed to make a great deal of difference.

Glenn nodded then, unsaddled Sky, and watched the big roan run low and swiftly along the pasture toward the dip trail to the river.

A deep contentment filled him. Sky was safe. Luce could buy cows to restock the *Shoestring*. And in the spring Glenn himself would enter Ames.

"Yes," he said, throwing an arm across Luce's shoulders and pulling him close, "a couple of pretty smart hombres, Luce. Now, let's go up and help Abbie get dinner for the gang."

Together, arm in arm, they moved slowly up the path to Abbie.

In the distance came the high shrill neigh of Sky, mingling with the caw of crows in the cottonwoods and the murmur of the distant river.